Angie Turner's Idaho restaurant, the County Seat, owes its success not only to its farm-fresh fare, but also to its devoted and passionate staff. And while murder is never on the menu, it often shows up as an uninvited guest . . .

A Pumpkin Spice Killing

At a much-deserved arts-and-crafts themed retreat, Angie and her County Seat staff find themselves helping an older guest uncover the whereabouts of his missing son . . .

Have a Deadly New Year

It's a rockin' New Year for Angie and her crew as they cater a bash for a famous band, but there are hints of discord when one of the musicians is found with a drumstick in his chest . . .

Penned In

The County Seat's crew goes on a quarterly out-of-office meeting at the Old Idaho Penitentiary near the Boise Foothills, a prison brimming with ghostly lore. The lock-in features actors role-playing as guards, fascinating prison stories . . . and an unscripted murder.

Visit us at www.kensingtonbooks.com
Mystery

A Basketful of Murder

A Farm-to-Fork Bundel

Lynn Cahoon

LYRICAL UNDERGROUND
Kensington Publishing Corp.
www.kensingtonbooks.com

The Farm-to-Fork Mysteries

Killer Comfort Food

Deep Fried Revenge

One Potato, Two Potato, Dead

Killer Green Tomatoes

Who Moved My Goat Cheese?

Novellas

A Pumpkin Spice Killing

Penned In

Have a Deadly New Year

The Tourist Trap Mysteries

Picture Perfect Frame

Murder in Waiting

Memories and Murder

Killer Party

Hospitality and Homicide

Tea Cups and Carnage

Murder on Wheels

Killer Run

Dressed to Kill

If the Shoe Kills

Mission to Murder

Guidebook to Murder

Novellas

A Very Mummy Holiday

Mother's Day Mayhem

Corned Beef and Casualties

Santa Puppy

A Deadly Brew

Rockets' Dead Glare

The Kitchen Witch Mysteries

One Poison Pie

Two Wicked Desserts

Novellas
Murder 101
Chili Cauldron Curse

The Cat Latimer Mysteries
A Field Guide to Homicide
Sconed to Death
Slay in Character
Of Murder and Men
Fatality by Firelight
A Story to Kill

To the extent that the image or images on the cover of this book depict a person or persons, such person or persons are merely models, and are not intended to portray any character or characters featured in the book.

This book is a work of fiction. Names, characters, businesses, organizations, places, events, and incidents either are the product of the author's imagination or are used fictitiously. Any resemblance to actual persons, living or dead, events, or locales is entirely coincidental.

LYRICAL UNDERGROUND BOOKS are published by
Kensington Publishing Corp.
119 West 40th Street
New York, NY 10018

All Kensington titles, imprints, and distributed lines are available at special quantity discounts for bulk purchases for sales promotion, premiums, fund-raising, educational, or institutional use.

Special book excerpts or customized printings can also be created to fit specific needs. For details, write or phone the office of the Kensington Sales Manager: Kensington Publishing Corp., 119 West 40th Street, New York, NY 10018. Attn. Sales Department. Phone: 1-800-221-2647.

First Electronic Edition: January 2023
ISBN-13: 978-1-5161-1035-3

A Pumpkin Spice Killing

A Farm-to-Fork novella

Chapter 1

Angie Turner leaned back in the shotgun seat in one of the two minivans she'd rented for the County Seat's most recent team building session. Hope Anderson, the restaurant's newest line cook, had been in charge of planning the session this quarter and she'd wanted to get the team building started as soon as the vans left the County Seat's parking lot.

"Pull the van into that coffee place and let's get something to drink. My treat." She pointed Ian McNeal, van driver and her boyfriend, to the upcoming coffeehouse. "I'll let Felicia know we're stopping at the drive-thru."

"Your wish." Ian grinned at her, then looked into the back of the van at Hope and Bleak Hubbard. They'd chosen to ride together in the front van with the addition of Dom, Angie's St. Bernard and County Seat mascot. The girls had become fast friends as soon as Bleak had arrived in River Vista. "You two old enough for coffee or should we get you hot chocolate?"

"I've been drinking coffee for years." Bleak tossed her hair back out of her eyes. She'd dropped the goth look, but her hair was still long and black. Now it had a healthy shine to it and Angie noticed she and Hope had matching pedicures with what looked like animals painted on the nails. "Anyway, get me a pumpkin spice latte. It's time to welcome fall."

"Yes, it is." Angie finished texting their stop to Felicia and, looking up from her phone, grinned at the newest member of the restaurant family. Bleak was still in high school, but she'd talked her school counselor into approving this community service trip even though it meant she'd miss three days of school. "I'll have the same. Large, please."

"You mean venti," Hope corrected her. "I'm in for the PSL too."

Ian shook his head. "Okay, three coffee light drinks and a real cup of coffee for me."

"Don't be that way. PSL is amazing." Hope curled her leg up underneath her and reached back to stroke Dom's back. He was back on the third seat sleeping. He lifted his head and gave Hope's hand a quick lick before plopping his head back down on the seat. "Does Dom need some water?"

"I gave him some before we left town and I've got a couple of bottles in that backpack on the floor. He'll let you know if he's thirsty." Angie loved how well Dom fit in with the group. He was as much of a family member as any of her staff.

"Depending on how many more stops I have to make, we should be there in about two hours." Ian glanced at the GPS he'd brought with him.

"Angie, do you think Matt bought that we were going to a knitting retreat?" Hope leaned forward toward the front of the van. "Did you see his face when I handed him the bag with yarn and knitting needles?"

"I thought the mini lesson/project sheet you gave him was awesome. He should be trying to figure out how to hold the needles right now. Nancy said she'd help him on the ride." Angie turned to face Hope. "When you set up a prank, you go all in."

"I can't believe he took us to a haunted prison last fall. It really wasn't fun. Especially after that guard was killed. If we make it through the next four days with no one dying, I'm calling this a success." Hope leaned back in her seat. "Especially when Matt finds out we're helping clean up this veteran's home instead of knitting."

"He's going to whine about that too." Bleak didn't look up from her fashion magazine. "Matt always whines when there's actual work to be done. I'm surprised Estebe hasn't moved him back to dishwasher as much as he complains about things."

"He's just young," Ian said as he pulled up to the speaker at the coffeehouse. "Hey, they have pumpkin bread too. Four slices?"

"Sounds like a plan." Angie opened her planner and started to make notes about the new menu she wanted to propose at the staff meeting they would have in a few days out at the farmhouse before they would pack up for home. She'd told the center's owner that the group would handle food for the center for the time they were there. She and Felicia would see what they needed and check for any specific dietary issues with the residents, then head to the local grocery store to stock the center's shelves.

They'd had to make the quarterly team building event smaller for the last few quarters, but this time, she was going all out. And she'd have time to test some of the recipes she wanted to propose.

Angie took the cups of pumpkin spice latte Ian handed her and passed two back to Hope and Bleak. She was getting into the road trip mood. The team building was going to be an amazing four days. Especially once Matt got over being tricked with the yarn.

By the time they reached River Vista Veteran's home, it was almost eleven. Angie got out of the van and took in the house and surrounding area. It was an old ranch-style home that needed a touch up. According to Hope, the woman who ran it, Mrs. Stewart, had been managing the center for over ten years. The house looked like it hadn't been painted in at least that long. The front yard needed weeding and grass planted. They had their work cut out for them.

Ian stood by her and whistled. "I didn't think it would be this bad. Hopefully the inside is better off, or we'll have to prioritize what we get done this time. I'll get my men's group to come out next month. We'll get this place ready for new residents. Don't worry."

"I didn't say I was worried," Angie responded.

He laughed and pulled her into a hug. "Honey, sometimes your face tells the whole story. It will be fine. I promise."

The other van pulled up and the rest of the crew joined them in front of the house. Matt stepped out and went to stand by Hope. "Wow. This place looks like it needs some work. Are you sure we're at the right place?"

"How's your knitting going?" Hope didn't look at him but Bleak snickered.

He glared at the young women. "This isn't a knitting retreat, is it? We're here to fix this place up."

"He gets it right on the first guess." Hope stepped forward to greet the woman who walked out of the house and onto the rundown porch. "Mrs. Stewart? I'm Hope Anderson and this is the County Seat crew. Angie and Felicia are our fearless leaders."

Angie and Felicia held up their hands.

"Well, isn't this nice. I so appreciate young people taking an interest in the people who served our country so many years ago. We have only two men in residence right now. Randy Owens and Kendrick Trickle. Both men saw the fall of Saigon and have a lot of stories to tell about their time. Randy's not been feeling well recently so he's probably not up to having visitors. It's sad when they're in the last days." Mrs. Stewart waved them forward. "Come on in, I'll show you your rooms."

"This is going to be an amazing few days." Hope took Bleak's hand and they were the first on the porch. Felicia and Angie exchanged a look and followed the crew into the house.

Yes, this was going to be an interesting team building session, Angie thought. She hoped that Bleak and Hope were up to the challenge. Although Angie didn't know why she was worried. Both of the young women came from families where service to others was something expected rather than just a once-a-year thing.

Mrs. Stewart stopped at a room and opened the door. "Girls room here. Boys will be on the other side of the hallway. I've left linens for the beds. I have iced tea and cookies in the parlor and I'll give you the to-do list. Now, don't think you have to get everything done in four days. Choose your projects. I'm sure God will send more helpers to our doorstep soon."

"My dad's men's group is planning a weekend to come up next month to help." Hope pointed toward Ian. "So you'll get to see that guy again. It's okay though, he's cool."

Mrs. Stewart smiled and nodded. "I've been talking to a third group out of River Vista who are coming soon. God really is good. Men, come this way and I'll show you your room."

Inside their room, Hope dropped her bag onto a top bunk. "Bleak, do you want top or bottom. Or you could have that top over there and we could talk?"

"Don't think you two girls are going to be chatting all night. I need my eight hours or I'm a bear. Just ask my kids." Nancy nodded to Angie. "Boss, do you want the single or do you and Felicia want the bottom bunks?"

"We'll take the bottom bunks." Felicia ran over to claim her bed. "This is so much fun. It's like camp."

"I don't know what camp you went to but we were in actual tents." Angie followed her over and motioned Dom to sit on the floor between the two bunks. "Let's get our beds made and stuff situated and then we can get busy. Daylight's wasting."

"Yes, mother," Felicia said behind her.

"I'd hit you with my pillow but I'm afraid it might break apart." Angie stuffed her pillow into a well-worn pillowcase with faded embroidery on the edge. "We may want to buy linens for the residents' rooms as our company Christmas charity."

"Great idea. I'll check it out and see what's needed." Felicia grabbed her phone and made a note.

Angie finished putting her clothes away in a drawer, then grabbed Dom's backpack and started unloading his stuff on top of the dresser. She put his canned food at the back and his bag of treats on top of that. Maybe he wouldn't sniff them out. "It's bad when I pack lighter for me than my dog, isn't it?"

"You spoil him." Felicia stood by the door. "Come on slowpoke. The girls are already heading to the living room for cookies."

Angie and Dom followed Felicia out but as she walked past a room, she heard a noise.

"Carol? Is that you?" A man's voice called out.

Angie glanced in the room and saw an elderly man sitting in a chair near the window looking outside. "Sorry, it's not Carol. My name is Angie Turner and this is my dog, Dom."

"He sure is a big fellow." The man reached out a withered hand and Dom went over to sit where the man could pet him.

Dom seemed to know when his services as a big fuzzy love puppy were needed. And this was one of those times. Angie moved closer so the older man could see her face. There was a metal folding chair near the wall, and she set it up so she could sit down for a minute. "How are you today? We're here to work on the house. I hope we won't be too noisy for you."

"Don't worry about me." The man grinned. "I'm only glad to have someone to talk to besides Carol. She means well, but she has a lot of work to do to keep all of us going. I'm Randy Owens. It's genuinely nice to meet you and Dom."

Angie noticed he hadn't taken his hand off the large dog's head and Dom didn't seem to mind at all. He had on the happy face that he got after they walked or went for a drive. "Did you have dogs?"

"All my life until I moved here. My last dog died a week before I fell and broke my hip. It's like he knew something was going to happen and didn't want me to worry about him. But I sure do miss Gideon." He absently stroked Dom's fur. "He was a Bernese Mountain dog. They don't live long lives, not like those yippy small dogs people carry around in their purse. I was lucky with Gideon, he survived fifteen years. Would have been sixteen that fall."

"That's a long time to be with a best friend." Angie reached out and touched Dom's face. "I hope I get twenty years out of this guy."

"You treat him right, you might."

"Angie, Angie Turner, are you back here?" A female voice called out from somewhere in the house.

"Sounds like you're being summoned." The grin made Randy's face look younger somehow. "And maybe you're in trouble. Carol doesn't like troublemakers."

Angie smiled and stood up, putting the chair back. "Then how are you still around?"

He chuckled and as they were leaving the room said, "You and Dom are always welcome to come visit me."

"Believe me, we'll be here so much, you'll get tired of seeing us." She paused at the doorway. Hadn't Carol said Randy was on his deathbed? The guy was old, sure, but he seemed to be coherent and alert. Maybe she'd been talking about the other resident.

"Miss Turner?" The woman called again, bringing Angie out of her thoughts.

"Coming." She was going to be spending more time with Randy. He loved dogs as much as she did.

Chapter 2

After they'd gotten a tour of the house and the crew had picked their three top projects, Angie and Felicia headed to the kitchen to get lunch started. Mrs. Stewart, or Carol, followed them. She pulled out a notebook from the bookshelf that held several recipe books.

"This is Randy's and Kendrick's dietary plan. There is a state dietician who comes quarterly to look at the food plan and make changes. She's been worried about Randy's weight lately, so she's backed off on some of the normal limitations. Mainly, she just wants him to eat. Kendrick is on a low-sugar diet due to his diabetes but other than that, you have free rein in planning meals." Carol handed the book to Angie. "Of course, if it's too much, I could just make them something separate from the main meal."

"We're chefs." Felicia took the book from Angie. "We're used to special requests for a dining room filled with people. Feeding this group is going to be a breeze."

"If you say so. I find it hard to find food they can eat and still taste good." Carol glanced out the door to where the guys were getting ladders out of the garage. "When it's busy, we eat a lot of oatmeal around here. Excuse me, I need to go help them find the third ladder."

Angie and Felicia shared a horrified look. Finally, Felicia glanced down at the notebook. "It doesn't say anything about using oatmeal as a replacement meal. The dietician says it can be used as a supplement if the residents are still hungry or find a meal not to their liking. She's using it to keep from cooking."

"Then we'll make up a batch of soups and casseroles to leave with her when we go. And I'll bring my testing extras out here a couple of times a month. My freezer is too full anyway." Angie took the notebook and closed it. "Let's get cooking. I think our residents might really need a good home-cooked meal."

Angie pulled out soup from the cooler that they'd brought for lunch the first day. "This Basque wedding soup should meet their dietary restrictions, right?"

"I think the only thing we're going to have to do is adjust the dessert recipes. We have fresh fruit I can make a salad out of for Kendrick. And we have brownies for the rest of the group. You get the soup warming up and I'll start making sandwiches." Felicia put her hair back into a ponytail and started working.

They were done just before one. Angie surveyed the trays they'd made for the residents and the rest of the food was set up buffet style for the others. "Should I ask if they want to come to the dining room and eat with us? According to Carol's notes, the residents eat in their rooms."

"That can't be fun." Felicia glanced around the room. "Hey, I'll go tell the others that food's ready and we can take the trays into the guys. Then we can sit with them for a while if they want us to."

"That's a good idea." Angie frowned as she looked at the lonely tray. "I'm going to put my soup on the tray too, that way I can sit and eat with Randy if he wants company."

"You're so smart." Felicia put a second bowl of soup on her tray as well. "I'll go sound the dinner bell and then take this in to Kendrick. See you after lunch."

Dom followed Angie to Randy's room. The older man was right where she'd left him, a book in his lap. She knocked on the door and he jerked awake. "I didn't mean to wake you, but I've got lunch."

"That smells wonderful. My late wife was a terrific cook. When I came home from being out of the country, I gained ten pounds in a month. Of course, we weren't eating too well that last few days before the city fell." He peered at the tray. "I may be hungry, but there's no way I can eat two bowls of that soup. I suspect you want to fatten me up while you're here."

"The second bowl is mine. I was wondering if you wanted company for lunch. I thought I might eat with you." She pulled a small table next to him and then set up the metal chair. As she did, Dom greeted the old man and then lay down next to his chair.

"I think your dog likes me."

"He's a good boy." Angie moved her soup closer toward her. "Eat before the soup gets cold."

"Now you do sound like my Mary Elizabeth." He smiled and picked up the spoon.

They were about halfway done with lunch when Carol came in, a tray in hand. "Oh, I didn't realize you'd already brought Randy his lunch. You don't have to do that."

"I wanted to. It's nice to share a meal with such wonderful company. Felicia's taken care of Kendrick's meal too." Angie set her spoon down near her bowl. "You should go eat. We'll handle this. You deserve a break."

"I usually give them their meds with meals." Carol wasn't giving up her status as head of the house easily.

"Did you forget the pills?" Angie studied the tray Carol held.

"What?"

"There's no bottles on the tray. Did you forget the pills?" Angie picked her spoon back up. "You can bring them in now if you want, but he doesn't need another food tray."

"Lord, no. I'm already stuffed." He scooped up the last of the soup with some of the bread from his sandwich. "But I'm still eating. Not to say bad things about your cooking Carol, but you really must try this soup. It's wonderful."

"My sous chef made it. It's his family recipe. We bring it out in the fall at the restaurant, but he always insists on making it himself. He won't tell anyone the recipe." Angie leaned closer. "I'm thinking he's using a premade soup base, but he swears it's all homemade. Well, as close as it can get in the restaurant."

"Well, I guess I'll come back with your pills." Carol turned and left the room.

He watched her go. "Carol's a nice lady but she really doesn't like people in her business. She wouldn't have asked for help if the state social worker hadn't told Carol if she didn't get the place up to code that the state was going to find other arrangements for Kendrick and me."

"I have to ask, how often does she feed you oatmeal for a meal other than breakfast?" Angie didn't look at Randy but she hoped he'd trust her with the truth.

"Now don't get that look on your face. Carol's doing the best she can. That's what we all do. Just the best we can." Randy covered a yawn.

"Do you want me to help you to your bed?" Angie set her empty bowl down and moved the table.

He shook his head. "I can make it. But there is one thing you can do for me."

"What?" Angie motioned to Dom to move out of the way. He came and sat by her feet, his head lolling on her thigh.

"Come back and talk to me later. I need a favor from you and I can't ask Carol. She gets a little testy around certain things." He shuffled to his bed, then turned around and sat. Carefully lifting his legs, he lay prone on the small mattress. "Just come back after my nap and I'll explain everything."

Angie carefully returned the chair, then grabbed the tray and motioned to Dom. He looked at Randy, then at her, then back to Randy. Angie slapped her leg and he moved toward the door. When they were out in the hallway, she reached down to pet his head. "I know you like your new friend, but he needs his sleep."

Dom glanced back at the room and whined low in his throat.

"What the heck?" Angie scratched behind his ears. "I've never known you to be this attached so soon."

"Attached to what?" Ian asked, coming down the hall. He'd taken ahold of the tray before he spoke, which was a good thing since Angie squeaked and about almost dropped it. "Whoa. You're freaked out about something. What's wrong?"

"Who. Dom's attached to and now nervous about his new friend." Angie handed Ian the tray and they turned to walk hand in hand to the kitchen, where they dropped off the tray, and then to the family room, where Carol was waiting for them. To face her wrath, Angie would need more than just a hoodie and a pair of running shoes.

"Thank you for lunch." Carol glared at Angie when she walked in. "I'm worried that your presence may upset the residents' schedule."

"I'm sure they could use some company." Ian sat on the couch and patted the seat for Angie to join him. "It must be hard being out here, isolated with just the three of you in the house."

"We have monthly visits from the social worker and a local nurse. And the dietician and doctor come quarterly," Carol sputtered.

"Yes, but that's paying people to talk to you. We're here on our own dime and spending time with your residents, just because it's the right thing to do." Ian nodded toward the group. "Maybe you should take advantage of our presence and take some 'me' time. We'll keep the place going."

Carol didn't quite know how to answer, at least judging from her facial expression. Angie had never seen a person that red before. *You got more than what you bargained for with this crew.* She wondered if Carol was just stubborn and stuck in her ways, or if something else was going on. "Hope, you and Bleak are on clean up kitchen duty. And if you're still there when I come back to start dinner, you can help me cook too."

"Sounds like a plan." Hope pulled Bleak onto her feet. The two girls paused, glancing at Carol, before they left the room. "Unless someone needs something else from us now."

"Nope, you're good." Felicia waved them away. "So glad we have the children along to do the dishes."

"I heard that. And I'm not a child," Hope called over her shoulder. A chuckle went around the room.

Angie sank back into the couch. "They grow up so fast. So what did you all get done this morning?"

"The walls are prepped outside and ready for a coat of paint, but I think we'll slow down outside and come in to do the room setup. I don't want to *need* to do this once a year." Estebe sat on the love seat, his big brawny arms curling around Felicia. "I think we may get more than three items off the to-do list."

"You could leave early if you get done before Sunday afternoon," Carol offered, a twinge of hope in her voice.

"Of course not! We'll just get more things done for you." Felicia seemed upset about the host's words, not for the first time. "There's nothing wrong with us staying around until Monday."

"Well, just remember if the residents start telling you about buried treasure or riding a motorcycle from San Diego to Seattle, it's a tall tale." Carol took two steps away from Matt, who'd snuck up behind her.

"Allowing them to tell us stories is the best medicine for a lonely heart. I intend to spend as much time as humanly possible with them. Besides, Dom loves Randy." Angie reached down and stroked his fur.

Carol pressed her lips together. "Well, just make sure you don't let him get overly tired. It's not good for him to go without his naps during the day."

Angie watched as the woman left the room, straightening a doily on the chair by the door as she walked by.

When the back door closed, Felicia shook her head. "That woman is wound as tightly as a grandfather clock."

"Are grandfather clocks on springs?" Matt asked Estebe. "I thought they had a pendulum system."

"That's not the point she's trying to make," Estebe responded.

Felicia sighed. "You know what I mean. The house isn't what I expected. Kendrick was scared to death to talk to me. Now, I know some men don't like talking to women, but he kept looking at the door, like he was afraid someone would overhear us and he'd be in trouble."

"I got the feeling Carol runs a tight ship, but I learned that she was forced to ask for help with the house by the state." Angie confided what Randy had told her. "Let's just keep our eyes out while we're here. It might be nothing."

Bleak stood at the doorway, shivering. "I overheard you talking. The place reminds me of home. We weren't allowed to talk to any strangers because you never knew who was with the state. We were told over and over that if the state came, they'd take us away from our parents and put us in an institution. With rats and gruel."

"Oh, sweetheart. I hope this isn't upsetting you." Ian stepped closer to the girl he now considered his cousin, even though she wasn't born into his family.

She lifted her chin. "As the great Gloria says, 'I will survive.'"

The room exploded with laughter and finally Angie stood. "Okay, we have our afternoon assignments. Keep your eyes open and work hard. This is for Randy and Kendrick, not for Carol. Just remember that."

As she and Bleak returned to the kitchen, Angie paused in the hallway. "Can we be serious for a minute? Are you okay?"

"I'm fine, really. When Felicia was talking about Kendrick, it struck a chord with me. I'm not saying it's the same as it is at the encampment where I lived, but it feels the same." Bleak narrowed her eyes and focused on a spot on the wall. "Does that even make any sense?"

Angie hugged her. "It does to me. And listening to your intuition is important. You see the world differently than the rest of us do. It's a good thing, believe me."

"Sometimes I wonder." Bleak turned into the kitchen and went back to the sink where Hope was washing dishes.

Bleak had grown up on a community farm in Utah. If Angie was being honest, probably in a cult. She'd handled her parents' household from a young age and was a hard worker. But when she'd been promised in marriage at sixteen, she'd run away to Idaho, where she'd wound up sleeping in the alley behind the County Seat. Ian had found her and taken her under his wing. Angie loved that about him. He was always looking out for others, no matter what the cost.

While Hope and Bleak were doing dishes, Angie started working on a shopping list for the center. She'd send Ian and Estebe to the store later this afternoon. She opened the pantry and started writing on her clipboard. The place needed everything. She leaned down and found pint jars filled with honey. The farm must have a beehive somewhere. Some of the jars still had honeycomb in them.

Smiling, she set the jars aside and kept working on the list. She found a trap door in the floor where potatoes, onions, and carrots were stored. She pulled out several and put them in one of the baskets stored nearby. A recipe for beef stew was forming in her head, if they had any meat to work with. She closed the root cellar door and looked around for a freezer.

Angie found it near the corner of the pantry. This room was huge and had plenty of shelf space. Carol just needed more food to put on the shelves.

When she opened the chest freezer, she found what looked like a side of beef all broken down to cookable pieces of meat. She found two packs of stew meat and pulled them out. Beef stew was what's for dinner. That and a nice cornbread to soak up the juices. She hadn't brought her cookbook, but this recipe she knew almost by heart. Besides, she had the ingredients on her phone as well since she and Felicia had been trying to finalize the recipes for the first annual County Seat cookbook.

She took the clipboard with the shopping list and the stew ingredients back into the kitchen. Hope was alone in the room drying the last few pans. "What did you find?"

"Actually, the freezer is well stocked. They need chicken but there's a lot of different cuts and types of meat and fish." Angie set the basket by the sink. "And there's a small root cellar to keep the vegetables fresh. Just not a lot of canned goods."

"Seems like the easy-to-cook and -serve items are always the first to go. Even at my parent's house." Hope eyed the ingredients Angie had brought out of the pantry. "There's a stock pot down here. I'll get it for you. I love stew."

Angie considered what she'd brought out as Hope found the pot. "I need another onion. And maybe there's some bones in the freezer for broth. Or even some packaged stuff. Right now I'm not picky."

She went back into the pantry and looked for the missing items. No bones and no broth. She'd have to make do. She dropped the onion she'd been carrying and ran over to get it. It had rolled into the pantry. She bent down and saw a box of rat poison on the floor under the food shelves. Angie picked it up by two fingers and took it into the kitchen. "Grab me a plastic shopping bag."

Hope got one and held it out. "Is this what you need?"

Angie slipped the box into the bag. Then she went to the sink to wash up. "I saw a shed out near the garden. Take that bag out there and tie up the top. Something like that should never be kept in a kitchen. I wonder why she wasn't cited for that before."

As Hope left out the back door, Angie started washing the potatoes. With such great produce around, she wondered how Carol didn't like to cook. Sometimes the quality of the ingredients made a huge difference in what came out of the kitchen. Of course, Ian ran the farmers market and didn't cook. When they'd met, he'd had what seemed to be a year's supply of canned spaghetti in his kitchen.

Chapter 3

With the stew slowly simmering in the kitchen and Hope and Bleak making cornbread, Angie had a few minutes to visit with Randy again. Dom hurried to the man's room and pushed open the door before she could open it.

"Well, hello little fella." Randy reached out to rub Dom's fur. "I'm so glad you could come back."

"Dinner's on the stove and I'm the only one without an assignment right now." Ian and Estebe had gone with Carol to find the local grocery store. Felicia had Matt and Nancy weeding the garden. "Did you have a nice nap?"

"The soup you made hit the spot. I haven't slept that deeply in months." Randy pointed to his end table. "Can you get the box out of that drawer for me?"

Angie walked over and got the box. Then she pulled the table closer and set the box on top where Randy could reach. She opened the metal chair and sat. "What's in the box?"

"Memories and regrets." Randy smiled at her, but he looked sad. "I need some help with a regret."

He took out a picture of a man and a woman and handed it to her. It was obviously their wedding day. The young man was in a dark suit and the woman in a modest wedding dress of white lace and satin, but the skirt ended at the knees. She wore a headdress with a puff of tulle on the back. They were both smiling.

"Beautiful couple. Who are they?" Angie set the photo back down on the table.

Randy picked the photo up again. "That's my son, Jacob, and the woman he married. Mai is her name. It's written on the back. The picture was in my wife's bible. I found it when she died."

"I don't understand. Didn't you know about the wedding?"

"Jacob brought her to meet us when he asked her to marry him. I was angry and stubborn. I told Jacob if he was going to marry one of *them*, he was disowned." He shook his head, tears in his eyes. "I spent years fighting the Vietnamese and he wants to marry this girl? Bring her into our family? I guess I was hurt that my time in the war didn't mean anything."

"But he married her anyway." Angie stated the obvious. "When did you last see him?"

"It's been over thirty years now." He set down the photo and looked out the window. "My wife, she kept in touch with them without letting me know. But I didn't even tell him when she died. I only had an old address I found later in her things. I should have told him his mother died. I guess when he didn't hear from her, he figured it out."

Angie let the words settle. This was Randy's story. He needed space to tell it.

"So now I'm an old man with a basketful of regrets at my feet. Can you help me fix this? Can you help me find my son?" Randy grabbed her hand and gently squeezed. "I'd ask Carol for help, but it's complicated. I need to know if he's alive. If he's happy."

"Of course." Angie pulled a piece of paper and a pen out of her pocket. "Tell me his name and where he lived the last time you knew. And his birthdate."

Randy gave her what he knew. Glancing at her watch, she saw she needed to get busy. "Sorry, dinner's coming up and I'm in charge tonight. I'll do some searching tonight and see what I can find."

"One favor. Please don't tell Carol. Like I said, she wouldn't understand. It's complicated." He stood and moved toward the bed. "I've got another nap to take before dinner. It's a tough job being this old."

Angie smiled and motioned to Dom to follow her. When she reached the kitchen he whined and stood at the back door.

"I'll get him," Bleak said as she opened the door. "I need a bit of a walk myself. Do I need the leash?"

"Please. And take a poop bag too." Angie washed her hands in the sink and laughed when Bleak wrinkled her nose. "Part of the fun of owning animals."

"I know." She grabbed the bag and tucked it in her shorts pocket, then clipped on Dom's leash. "Come on, big boy, let's go stretch our legs."

Hope pulled a pan of cornbread out of the oven. "She loves dogs. They weren't allowed to have pets at the compound. And she hasn't brought it up to the Browns yet."

"She only has one more year before she goes away to college. Can't really take a dog to the dorms." Angie cut a slice of the cornbread. She tasted it without butter or anything else. "Yum. This is really good. You guys did great."

"Thanks. I love making cornbread to go with stews and soups in the fall. My mom will bake bread some weekends, but I like the ease that cornbread has. Not so labor intensive." Hope cut a piece off and popped it into her mouth. "Bleak and I have been talking about renting a house in Boise maybe when she goes to school. She'll be working and I think renting will be cheaper than living on campus. And the thought of living in the dorms, well, it kind of scares her. Too many people."

Angie studied the young woman who'd started working for her as a dishwasher, the job Bleak took over when Hope moved to line chef. "Is that something you'd want?"

"I need to get out of the house. My folks are driving me crazy. Their house, their rules. You know the drill. And I like Bleak. We'd have fun together. I think Maggie's going to be upset if she doesn't try to rush a sorority, but she's just not into the normal college life." Hope looked around the kitchen. "How do you want to serve dinner?"

"Let's dish out bowls of stew and put them on a plate with two squares of cornbread. Then we'll put a generous pat of butter on the plate and more butter on the sideboard, just in case they want more. Do you think that will work?" Angie surveyed the room. "Then we can eat out on the deck or in the dining room."

"Are you eating with Randy again?" Hope pulled out bowls from the cabinet and set them near the stove and the stewpot.

"Actually, I think I'll ask Ian to sit with him. He might like to chat with a guy for a while rather than me." Angie looked out the back screen door and saw the van pull up. "Besides, I'm going to be busy putting away groceries."

Hope followed her gaze. "Cool, they're back. I'm starving."

"Let's get the stew dished out and then we'll eat. I'll put away the perishables and come sit with you and Bleak." Angie dished out the first bowl. "I'd like to hear more about this renting plan. Have you talked to Estebe? He might have a place for you that he'd let you rent."

"Great idea." Hope cut cornbread and set it on the plate, one square halfway on top of the other, resting on the plate. She put the butter on the left side of the bread and put a spoon and a butter knife on the plate. "How's this?"

"Perfect. And easy to pick up and move." She nodded to the two trays behind them. "Set up the trays with two meals and I'll send Ian and Estebe in to eat with Kendrick and Randy. I think we'll all take a turn with meal duties."

"Sounds good to me." Hope grinned as the men came into the kitchen, arms filled with grocery bags. "Welcome back. You're just in time for dinner."

"Good, because I'm starving." Ian sniffed the air. "Your beef stew. I'm in heaven."

"I'm glad you're in a good mood because you and Estebe are taking trays in to the residents. They need someone to talk to who has the Y chromosome." She pointed to the table near the inside wall. "Just set everything over there. I'll get it put away as soon as I eat."

Estebe held up a bag. "I'll put the items that need to be refrigerated over here to the left of the table."

"Perfect." Angie nodded to Carol as she came into the kitchen. Her oversized tote was over one shoulder and she carried one grocery bag. "I bet you're starving too, after having to deal with them at the store."

"They were fine. Perfect gentlemen." She noticed the filled bowls on the trays. "You're giving the residents way too much to eat. Their tiny stomachs can't eat two bowls full."

"Actually, the extra bowls are for Estebe and Ian. They're just getting the groceries inside, then they'll take their food along with them." Angie took the grocery bag from Carol and set it down on the table.

"I can't have you all just popping in on them all the time. They need their privacy," Carol protested.

"Men need other men to talk to," Estebe said as he picked up one of the trays. "It's the way of the world. We are here, we need each other's counsel."

Ian, Angie, and Carol watched as Estebe took the tray and headed toward Kendrick's room. Ian shrugged and picked up the other tray. "There are only a few more bags in the van. Can you send Hope and Bleak out to get them?"

"I'll get them." Bleak came into the house and let Dom off his leash. "I dropped his present, bag and all, into the outside trashcan. I figured you didn't want it in here."

"I'll help." Hope started to take off the plastic gloves she'd been wearing to set up the cornbread.

"Stay here and finish the dinner service. It won't take me more than two trips. I peeked in the back when I walked by." Bleak headed back outside.

Ian leaned over and gave Angie a quick kiss. "Talk with you later, okay?"

"Sounds good." Angie dished up another bowl of stew. "Are you ready to eat, Carol?"

Carol watched Ian until he disappeared into Randy's room. Finally, she sighed and turned back toward the counter. "I can't wait."

Hope handed her a completed plate and Carol left the kitchen and headed to the other side of the house. Angie assumed her living area was on that side. She dished up another bowl of stew. "How many more do we need?"

"Six," Hope said as she took the plate and put cornbread on it. "Five now. I get the feeling Carol's not too happy with having us here."

"She's not hiding her feelings very well." Angie dished up another bowl. "I wonder why she's so insistent on us staying away from Randy and Kendrick?"

"That is the question, isn't it?" Hope focused on setting the cornbread on the plate just right.

Angie finished dishing out the bowls, then texted Felicia that dinner was ready. "I'm sitting outside to eat. What about you?"

"Sounds great." Hope grabbed her plate and held the door open for Bleak to bring in the last of the bags.

"Except I forgot that I have to put away the perishables." Angie sighed and set down her plate. She went over to the table and started pulling out the items that needed refrigeration. Hope and Bleak picked them off the table and put them in the fridge. Angie cocked her head, studying the girls. "I thought you two were going to eat?"

"I will as soon as you sit down too. Many hands make light work." Hope smiled at her boss. "One of my mother's favorite sayings. Along with Jesus helps those who help themselves."

In just a few minutes, not only were the perishables put away, but so was all the food and even the paper products. Angie glanced around in pleasure. "Light work done."

The girls grabbed their dinners and headed outside to the deck. Felicia, Matt, and Nancy came in from the garden with their arms loaded with a pile of peppers and some late-season tomatoes. Felicia motioned for them to put the haul on the sink. "Look what we found."

"We'll meal-plan them into tomorrow's schedule." Angie pointed to the kitchen. "Come out and sit and eat with me. I've sent your fiancé off to eat with Kendrick."

"Sounds great. And I love it when you say fiancé. It sounds so French," Felicia said before heading into the kitchen.

Angie ate some of the stew. It was perfect. Of course, a different version would have had some red wine, which would have given the stew a different flavor profile.

She heard Felicia sit next to her. "I can't believe that garden. It's huge. But it looks abandoned. Like someone just stopped taking care of it."

"Carol doesn't seem like the gardening type. Maybe someone else used to live here." Angie leaned close and quietly told Felicia about her talk with Randy. "Can you help me do some research tonight?"

"Of course. We'll hide in our room and work on the secret project. This is turning out to be more and more like camp." Felicia tasted the cornbread. "This is so good, you don't even need the butter. Good job."

"Give the praise to Hope and Bleak. Those two are becoming quite good in the baking department." Angie polished off one of her squares. "You might not need to be the pastry chef soon."

"I like being the pastry chef." Felicia grinned. "It gives me permission to taste-test all the desserts. But it wouldn't be a bad idea to train a backup."

"Especially since you'll be gone for a month on your honeymoon next summer." Angie watched the sun starting to set in the western sky. One day down and she already had a mystery to solve. Maybe Ian was right. She might just be attracted to these investigations like a fly to honey.

"I can't believe I'm getting married next year. I always thought you would be first." Felicia leaned into Angie, hitting Angie's shoulder against her own. "Of course, I was praying Todd wouldn't ask you. He was just along for the gravy train. He never would have been committed."

"I don't disagree. Todd was a mistake from day one." Angie smiled at an old memory. One where Todd, Felicia, and she were tubing the Boise River. Todd had been fun. But when there was work to be done, he always had somewhere else to be. Kind of like a reverse Clark Kent and Superman.

"I don't think I've ever heard you say that and actually mean it." Felicia leaned back in her chair, looking up to the darkening sky. "It's such a lovely night. I'm so glad Hope set this retreat up. Of course, we need to sit down together maybe tomorrow and talk about the plans for County Seat's next year. I love thinking about all the possibilities."

"You make it sound like the restaurant's a living thing." Angie laughed as she finished her cornbread. "I do think we should do more volunteer activities like this and the time we served at the homeless shelter."

"I'm not sure I could get Estebe to agree to that. He's still a little miffed at the way Taylor treated our relationship." Felicia lifted up her left hand

and stared at the engagement ring. Taylor and Felicia had been dating when the teambuilding outing had been at the homeless shelter Taylor ran. The relationship hadn't lasted long, especially after Felicia realized she was more arm candy for the center's fundraising events than girlfriend. "But maybe we could think about the food bank or the women's shelter."

"We could make our team outings a service project." Angie was getting excited about the options.

"Some of the time. The crew needs fun too," Felicia said.

Angie scoffed. "This isn't fun?"

"You were cooking all day. To you, cooking is fun. The rest of us were scraping paint and cleaning out the garden. Which still needs some work tomorrow," Felicia reminded her.

"Estebe said he wanted to be on the home projects, not cooking, but I guess I could switch out with Nancy or Matt." Angie had already been planning tomorrow's meals, but she could hand the kitchen over.

"Don't look like that. I'm giving you crap. Nancy wants to be on the garden crew this week and Matt, he's already started setting up the painting supplies to start tomorrow. The kitchen is yours. But you need to realize that the crew is really working hard."

"Angie knows this," Estebe said as he came out the kitchen door. "She is working hard to make delicious food for these war veterans. Kendrick said that the two meals she made was the best food he's had in years."

"That's the kind of compliment that keeps me cooking." She stood and picked up her plate. She reached for Felicia's plate. "Are you done?"

"Yes. The stew was lovely." Felicia glanced toward the kitchen. "Can I help you clean up?"

"I was hoping we could go for a walk down the road for a few minutes," Estebe said, glancing at Angie. "We haven't had a minute alone all day."

"You're such a romantic. Go ahead and take a walk. I've got a lot of people here who can help me wash dishes." Angie watched as Estebe held out his hand to help Felicia up out of the chair. They were a great couple and were going to build an amazing family. She moved into the kitchen and started working. Matt, Hope, and Bleak dropped their plates off and started out the door. "Where are you off to?"

"There's a pond down the road we want to check out. There's fishing poles in the garage and Randy says he used to catch trout in the pond." Matt grabbed a cookie off the plate on the counter. "I might just catch us enough for dinner tomorrow."

"Fishing's gross, but I'd love to see the pond. Maybe wade a bit in the water." Bleak moved around Matt and took two cookies, giving one to Hope.

Hope glanced at the dishes. She didn't follow the other two out of the house. "Do you need help with cleaning up from dinner?"

"No, you go ahead and have fun. I'll get these. Besides, Nancy and Ian are still around." Angie started stacking the plates and bowls.

"Actually, Nancy's in her room. She said she needed to call her kids and make sure they were following the rules for her mom, who's babysitting. I can stay and help." Hope glanced around, realizing that the pool of possible helpers for Angie was dwindling with each word out of her mouth.

"No, go ahead and have fun. I can do dishes." Angie waved a towel at Hope. "They're going to leave without you."

She shook her head. "No, they aren't. I was the one who talked to Randy about the pond. I popped into his room this afternoon to chat a little. He reminds me of my grandfather. He's in Oregon with my aunt, so I don't get to see him much. Anyway, Bleak and Matt don't know where it is so they have to wait for me. Thanks for cleaning up, Angie."

"We all have our jobs." Angie started the water and watched Hope glance around one more time, then she took off after her friends.

"I thought she'd never leave." Ian came in with the tray from Randy's room. "Randy's gone to bed and I'm reporting for kitchen duty."

"Are you sure you know the drill?" Angie took the plates from the tray.

He put the bowls by the others and then took a washcloth and soaked it in the soapy water. "I do. I was a professional dishwasher once. Well, for about a week, but nothing seems to have changed. Besides, we need to talk."

"Why, is something wrong with Randy?" Angie studied Ian's face as she put the silverware in the soapy water.

"No, but the pastor of Hope's church got a call from Carol about an hour ago. She told him that we weren't working out." Ian cleaned the other tray. "Angie, she wants us to leave the center."

Chapter 4

"What are you talking about? We're only scheduled here for three more days and the house isn't even painted yet." Angie dropped the plates into the sink and started washing them. "This doesn't make any sense."

"I know. And the pastor said we should stay here. He was just letting me know there's a bit of controversy going on. He talked her down. I guess he works with the social worker who's been assigned to the center from the state. If Carol doesn't let us help get this place up to code, she's going to lose her license and Randy and Kendrick will be moved to other places. Maybe that would be for the best, but I think something else is going on that Carol's afraid we'll find out."

"Why does she only have two residents?" Angie dropped her voice as she glanced around the kitchen. It wouldn't do for Carol to walk in on their conversation. "Do you know?"

"There were three, but one of the men died a month ago. The county sheriff called it old age, but the social worker was suspicious. She's asked for an autopsy, but since he's already been buried and had no relatives, she has to get a court order."

Angie thought about the rat poison in the pantry. She pushed the thought away. No one would be that cruel. "Carol wouldn't kill anyone. Would she?"

"We just need to keep together and keep her out of the kitchen while we're here. The social worker is working on finding out what really happened. If she's right, whatever killed this guy was slow acting. That's why the sheriff thinks it was his heart. The local doctor thinks he just went in his sleep." Ian put the plates he'd dried up in the cabinet. "I don't like gossip, but maybe she's onto something here."

"I just can't see a motive. This is her livelihood. She needs the residents to get paid for their care." Angie washed the last pot and after rinsing it, grabbed her own towel. "What was the man's name?"

"Phil O'Conner. I called Uncle Allen a few minutes ago and asked him to look into the place and any unexplained deaths." Ian stared down at the bowl he was drying when he added, "He says hi by the way."

"More like he said I can't believe she fell into another mystery. *What is with your girlfriend?* Something like that?" Angie knew Ian was telling a white lie because he had a tell. He didn't look at her when he lied. And he lied very badly. It just wasn't in his nature to be untruthful. "Anyway, I've got another project if you want to help me tonight."

"Finding Randy's son?" Ian finished drying the bowls. "Let's grab our laptops and a notebook and go outside with some hot chocolate. I think it's still light enough for a few hours for us to get a good start on it."

"He told you?" Angie ran the washcloth over the cabinets and stove. Tomorrow she was going to clean the oven as well as give the kitchen a deep clean. Even if Carol didn't want them there, she wouldn't be able to fault their work ethic.

"He did. He has a bit of a crush on you. I had to tell him you were my girl to get him to stop praising your kindness." Ian looked around the kitchen. "Everything washed and dried?"

"As far as I can tell. Let me grab Dom's bowl and some water and maybe he'll stay around the patio without being on a lead."

"Miracles do happen." Ian leaned over and kissed her. "Uncle Allen means well."

"I know. I'm probably touchy on the subject because he isn't wrong. I tend to fall into these things, but this one was so not my fault. Hope set up the team building. All I've done is pay the bills." She headed to her room to grab her notebook and her laptop. Dom followed her but then went past the room and sat in front of Randy's doorway. Angie went to get him and stared in at the elderly man. He was asleep in his bed, his hands over the cover and a smile on his lips. Angie grabbed Dom's collar and led him away from the room. She didn't want to wake him up, but she couldn't stop herself from wishing him good night. "Sweet dreams, Randy."

She gathered her stuff and found Ian already outside. Two cups of cocoa were sitting on the table, whipped cream on the top. "That was fast. I take it it's instant?"

"I'm not the chef." Ian grinned. "The whipped cream will help it taste better."

"As long as I didn't have to make it, I don't care." She filled Dom's water dish and then sat next to Ian. Dom positioned himself between the door to the house and them. She called his name and pointed out toward the garden and yard area. "The threats are going to be this way, buddy."

Dom glanced at her, then turned away and faced the door.

"He's not having the best retreat. He seems reserved. I've never seen him so quiet." Angie frowned as she watched her dog. "You don't think he's sick, do you?"

"No, he seems fine. Maybe a little subdued, but there are other people here. Maybe he's just overwhelmed." Ian reached down and scratched the top of Dom's head. "You okay, buddy?"

The question got a short bark in response, then Dom laid his head down again.

"Well, I guess we were told."

Ian looked at her, surprise in his eyes. "And what exactly do you think he told us?"

"That he's doing what he needs to do and to stop talking about him. It makes him crazy. He said you should know what he's thinking by now." Angie booted up her laptop and opened her search engine.

"You got all that from a bark?" Ian followed suit, watching her carefully.

Angie laughed. "You didn't? Seriously, you need to bone up on your dog translation skills. Bone up, get it?"

"It's not funny if you have to explain the joke." He leaned into his computer. "This is interesting."

"What did you find?"

"There's a Jacob Owens in Boise. Not sure if he's married or not, but it lists a phone number. He's a carpenter." Ian pulled out his phone and dialed a number. He grimaced and whispered, "Voice mail."

Angie listened to the generic message Ian left, and after he was finished she nodded to the notebook. "Write down the number and what you found. We'll may have to wait until tomorrow for a callback since that was probably his work number."

"I was hopeful." Ian picked up the pen and wrote a note.

Angie giggled. "Seriously, you thought you'd solve this mystery with five minutes on the internet and a phone call?"

"It could happen." Ian went back to searching. Angie found the next possibility and they went like that for the next hour.

They had ten names or variation of names on the list when they stopped. Angie closed her notebook and tapped the pen on the paper. "Maybe Randy and his wife lived other places when they were raising Jacob. He could have gone back to one of those areas. Randy was in the military."

"Military brats move around a lot." Ian nodded. "Good point. I'll write a note to ask Randy tomorrow."

"I'll take breakfast." Angie closed the notebook and set it on top of the closed laptop. Voices were coming up the road. Soon, out of the darkness, she could see Matt, Hope, and Bleak. Matt was carrying a fishing pole, but from what Angie could see, no fish. The girls were chatting a few steps behind. "Hey guys, want some hot chocolate?"

"Actually, I'm going to grab a shower and head to bed. I'm beat." Matt walked over to the shed and put the pole and fishing items inside. "No fish, but I got a few bites. Then my line kept getting snagged. Anyway, I'm going out again tomorrow night, just in case."

"Sounds fun." Angie turned to the girls. "What about you two? Hot chocolate?"

"Definitely, but we're making brownies too so we can make our own. You guys stay out here and relax." Hope shared a look with Bleak as they went inside, Matt following.

"Okay, so what was that look for?" Ian reached over and took Angie's hand in his.

Angie shook her head. "With those two? It could have been anything. Felicia said they've both been really involved in the wedding prep. I'm so glad she has someone to help her because if she depended on me, they would elope."

"You aren't a party planner. You never have been. That's Felicia's specialty." Ian nodded to the garden. "Do you think there's enough light to go for a short walk?"

"It's beautiful. Let's go." Angie picked up the leash and clicked it on Dom's collar and the three of them walked around the house and out to the country road. "Without road lights it's going to get dark quick out here."

"Sunset is an hour away. We'll walk for twenty, then turn back." Ian took Dom's lead and put his arm around Angie. "We'll be fine."

That night, Dom's barking woke Angie up in the middle of a nightmare. She couldn't remember what she'd been dreaming about, but the fear from the dream was still with her. She grabbed her phone and used its flashlight to find her slippers. Dom wasn't sleeping between her and Felicia. "Dom?" She called quietly

She shone the light on Felicia's bed. No Dom. She started to worry. She got up and searched the room using the small light. He wasn't on Nancy's bed either. Maybe he'd gone to find Ian in the middle of the night. He'd stopped barking. Or maybe she'd dreamed it.

She stepped into the hallway and saw him. He lay in front of Randy's room, blocking the doorway with his body. He lifted his head when he heard her approach and his tail gently thumped on the floor.

"Hey boy, what are you doing out here? Playing guard dog?" She reached down to rub his head and he licked her hand. Angie glanced into the room. Randy appeared still to be in bed, even though all she could see in the dim light of the nightlight in his bathroom was a man-sized lump under the covers. She shivered in the chilly hallway. Something had her dog freaked out about his new friend. Tomorrow she was going to call this social worker and see what she knew. She didn't feel right just packing up in three days and leaving Randy here. Especially if the last resident hadn't died of natural causes.

She went back into her room and lay there wide eyed, listening to the house sounds. Sometime during the night sleep had taken her back, and now Felicia was gently shaking her awake.

"Time to get up. I've made coffee and a batch of cinnamon rolls are in the oven." Felicia tsked as she studied Angie's face. "You don't look like you got any sleep last night. Maybe you should try for a few more hours."

Angie kicked the covers off. "No rest for the wicked. I'm grabbing a shower. Can you cut up some fruit to go with the cinnamon rolls? I'll make eggs for everyone as soon as I get dressed."

"Ian and Estebe ran into town." Felicia dropped her voice. "The social worker wanted to talk to them. Ian caught us up this morning. It's kind of chilling to be in a house where a murder might have taken place."

Angie took her friend by her shoulders. "It's worse when the murderer might be in the house with us. Just keep this to yourself, but make sure everyone stays in pairs. Buddy system and no one leaves the property without telling someone. Make sure the rest of the team knows as well."

"Hope's going to be devastated if this trip turns into a murder mystery too. She's still giving Matt grief about the fiasco at the penitentiary." Felicia took several deep breaths. "Okay, I'm okay. Everything's okay. It's going to be okay."

"New mantra?" Angie watched as Felicia visibly calmed down.

"New yoga teacher. She says situations are as much about how you approach them as the actual event. So now I'm going to assume the best out of everything and everyone. Then bad things won't happen." Felicia shrugged. "Or at least that's the hope."

"Stranger things have happened." Angie picked up her bathroom kit and clean clothes for the day. "I'll be quick."

"Just be careful." Felicia smoothed the comforter on her bed. "Nancy's in the kitchen drinking coffee. I'll go talk to her first."

"Don't worry anyone. Just let them know to be cautious." Angie didn't want her team freaking out. She ran into Dom in the hallway. He was standing by the doorway now, but when he saw Angie, he sat at attention. "Hey big guy. Can you wait a minute and I'll take you out after my shower?"

The squirm at the word out told Angie the answer was probably no. Matt came out of the other bedroom.

"Hey Angie. Does Dom need a walk?" He reached down and rubbed Dom's head.

"Would you please?" Angie held up her full hands. "I've got to get a shower still."

"No problem." Matt slapped his leg. "Come on big guy, let's go outside."

Dom followed Matt, but before he left the hallway, he turned back and looked at Randy's room. *Message received. You're still worried about him.* Angie glanced inside and Randy was sitting in his chair, reading.

She hurried to the bathroom, hoping that nothing would happen during her quick shower. If it did, her dog might not forgive her.

It took ten minutes but by the time Angie had finished getting ready, she walked by Randy's room and Ian was sitting with the man. Coffee cups were on the table. She caught his gaze and he waved at her. Hurrying, she dropped her stuff off on her bed and then went into the kitchen.

Everyone else in the house seemed to be there, except Carol, Kendrick, and Nancy. She stepped next to Felicia as she finished cutting up strawberries. "Is Nancy with Kendrick?"

"She just took him some coffee. They're talking about her kids. He has grandkids that age." Felicia smiled and then turned away from the others. "Carol's in the living room talking to the doctor."

"Why's a doctor here?" Angie tried to glance into the room, but she couldn't see anything.

"She said it's his monthly visit. I think she's trying to get him to say we're too much distraction for Randy and Kendrick." Felicia glanced around the room where Hope and Bleak sat talking with Estebe. "She really doesn't like us here."

"Well, I think she and the doctor need some coffee and cinnamon rolls." Angie dished up two of the rolls that Felicia had cooling on the stove. Then she poured three cups of coffee, and added a cream and sugar set and spoons. Picking up the tray, she nodded to Felicia. "Wish me luck."

She didn't pause at the doorway, just came right in the room and set the tray down on the table. Then she held her hand out to the doctor. "Good morning. I'm Angie Turner, owner of the County Seat over in River Vista. My kitchen crew is here working with Carol to get the home set up for new residents this fall."

"Nice to meet you. Carol was just telling me about you and your crew. I'm Ollie Norton. I'm the resident doctor for the area. I have an office over on the south side of Nampa." He took a whiff of the cinnamon rolls. "Carol, you must be in heaven having your own personal chef for a few days."

Carol mumbled something, but Angie didn't think it was agreement.

Angie turned her smile on Doctor Ollie. "Do you want a cinnamon roll? Tomorrow we're doing pumpkin donuts. Kind of a tribute to the season."

"I'd love one. And you brought out coffee. How nice." He beamed at her, then his grin dropped as he saw Carol's glare.

"I brought a cup for me as well." Angie set the rolls and coffees in front of Ollie and Carol and then the cream and sugar. She set the tray on the floor near her and sat in the wing chair next to the coffee.

"This is a private conversation," Carol said.

Angie nodded. "I know all about patient-doctor privilege, and I'll let you get back to that, but first I have some questions for the doctor."

"I'll try to answer, but Carol's right, my hands are tied on my patients." He dug his fork into the roll and took a bite. Angie could almost hear the groan he didn't let out. Felicia's cinnamon rolls were legendary.

"Okay, I was going to ask you about Randy. He seems a little depressed. I'd like to continue to visit after this week and I was wondering what you thought about me coming by with some baked goods. I noticed he doesn't have a lot of dietary limits." Angie sipped her coffee and watched Carol react to the news.

"I think that would be fabulous. Especially if you could get him to eat more. He's lost so much weight in the last few months. It's troubling." Ollie wiped his mouth with a napkin.

"You can't tell her that," Carol shrieked.

He stared at her. "Calm down, Carol. I can make statements that generalize my client's state. I didn't tell her how much weight he's lost or the percentages. I believe I'm the doctor here, correct?"

"Yes, Ollie." Carol went white. She picked up her coffee but ignored the cinnamon roll.

"That would be great. I'll put a visit on next month's schedule." Angie smiled at Carol. "This will be so fun. You won't know when I'm going to pop in."

Carol's face went even whiter, which had been Angie's intent.
Ian ran into the room. "You're the doctor?"
Doctor Ollie rose to his feet. "Yes, I am. What's wrong?"
Ian met Angie's gaze. "Something's wrong with Kendrick. Hurry."

Chapter 5

"Do you think one of us should go to the hospital to check on Kendrick?" Felicia and Angie were sitting in the kitchen at the center. Breakfast had been cooked and eaten. Dishes were washed and put away. The rest of the crew was in the garden or had started painting the outside of the house.

Angie shook her head. "No. It would look weird. Maybe we can take him flowers tomorrow. We have stuff to do here and only two more days to get it done."

"I can't believe how fast he got sick. Nancy said he was talking about his family and all of a sudden, it was like he'd had a seizure. I'm glad I wasn't in the room with him. I would have freaked out. Nancy was calm and collected. She stabilized Kendrick, called for Ian, and kept her cool during the whole thing." Felicia leaned back in her chair. "Okay, Angie, what's going on? You're too quiet and not feeding into or feeling my whole conspiracy theory."

"You haven't laid out a theory yet." Angie stood and got the pot to refill Felicia's coffee. "But I have to admit, he seemed fine yesterday. Can I tell you something else weird?"

"Of course." Felicia pulled in closer. "What do you know?"

"I don't know anything. I found Dom out in the hallway last night after everyone went to bed. You're going to think this is strange, but Dom appeared to be guarding Randy's room. And this morning, Randy's not sick like he says he's been, but Kendrick is. What if someone was going to give something to Randy, but Dom wouldn't let them?"

"That's probably pushing the limit for believability." Felicia looked around the kitchen. "Hey, where is Dom? Did someone take him out?"

Angie stood and motioned Felicia to follow. When they reached Randy's room, they saw Dom lying by the man's chair. Randy's hand was on Dom's fur and he seemed to be reading aloud to the dog.

Felicia started to say something, but Angie shook her head and pointed back to the kitchen. When they sat back down, she picked up her coffee cup. "The only times I've seen Dom act like that is when Ian's told him I was in danger and he had to watch out for me. I swear, Dom knows something bad has been happening to Randy and doesn't want it to happen again."

Felicia shrugged. "You could be right. Anyway, have you found Randy's son yet?"

Angie shook her head. "We have some calls out, but so far, nothing."

"Let me do some checking. I'll be right back with my laptop." Felicia stood and started to walk out toward the hallway.

"Bring my notebook too," Angie called after her. She studied the meal plan for the day. She needed to get some work done on the pantry as well. She wanted everything here to be as safe as possible. Even though she still didn't think Carol was doing this on purpose, she didn't want to take any chances.

As if she'd been pulled from Angie's nightmare, Carol appeared in the doorway.

"I don't know what game you're playing, but you need to realize I've been playing games a lot longer than you or any of your crew," Carol croaked.

"I'm not sure what you're talking about, but I wanted to get your take on an apple pie for dessert."

"You're not fooling me, missy." Carol came closer and Angie could see the crazy in her eyes. "You and your friends need to do your job and then get the heck out of here, never to return."

"Oh, but Doctor Ollie said…"

"I don't care what that old quack says. This is my house, my rules." Carol turned and left the kitchen. "I'm running to town on an errand. Please don't burn down the house while I'm gone."

"So apple pie?" Angie called after her as Felicia came back into the kitchen.

Felicia set her computer down. "What was that about?"

"I think Miss Carol is getting tired of us being here. We know the social worker won't help her kick us out. Now she lost the doctor from her side. I wonder what she's trying to hide." Angie opened her notebook and started making notes.

"If the social worker has the power to get Carol to make changes, do you think she has a contract with the state for the home?" Felicia tapped her pen on the table. "We had to go through all kinds of licenses and such to open the restaurant. I wonder if it's the same for homes for the elderly."

"I saw a license in one of the cabinets. Hold on." Angie glanced around then went to the top cabinet over the stove. A folder filled with papers sat there. She pulled it down. "Go and see if Carol's car is still in the driveway. I'd hate to have her come back while we're snooping through her stuff."

Felicia went and stood at the living room window. "She's just leaving now. Well, she's in the car talking on her phone. Wait, she's pulling out and heading down the road towards Nampa."

"Watch for a few minutes and make sure she doesn't turn around." Angie grabbed the folder and took out her phone. She found a license that expired the next December. Felicia had been right. The home was certified. Next was a letter from the state about the deficiencies they found during an annual inspection. She snapped pictures of all the pages and of the license, then what must have been the original contract with the state. And there was another bunch of papers from the Veteran's Administration. Angie glanced through to find a contact name on that stack.

"She's gone. And I have Matt watching for her to return. What did you find?" Felicia said from her left.

"Lots of paper." Angie handed Felicia the stack from the VA. "Can you take pictures of that pile? Looks like I've got a lot of reading to do in the next day or so."

"How are you going to do that and help Randy find his son?" Felicia shook her head. "Let me and Estebe work on this in between our chores here. You and Ian focus on Randy's mystery. I'll figure out what's going on with Carol and the home. Divide and conquer."

"Sounds like a plan. I'll send you the stuff I take pictures of after we get this file gone through."

They worked for over ten minutes before everything had been photographed and copied into Felicia's phone. On the back of the file, she found a note. "There's a name and phone number on the folder. I'll take a picture of it too. Maybe it's another social worker."

Matt came into the kitchen from the back door. "She's coming down the road. Whatever you're doing, you need to be done."

Angie snapped the last picture, then they put all the papers back into the folder and put it away. Then she got out the flour and butter and a bowl. "Felicia, can you start peeling those apples?"

"Of course, but why?" Felicia went over and washed her hands. Then she lifted the colander full of apples out of the sink and put a grocery sack into the empty sink for the peels.

"I told her we were making apple pie. I want to at least look like I wasn't lying." Angie grinned at her friend. "Besides, once I get this done, I can start going through the cabinets and cleaning and restocking. Maybe there's something else of interest in there."

"I'll go out and work in the garden after I get these peeled and cut. Unless you need me for lunch?" Felicia was making short work of the apples.

Angie started mixing the pie dough. "No, we'll do soup and sandwiches again. I think I'm going to have the guys barbeque some hamburgers tonight and we'll do a couple of salads to go with it."

"There's a few melons out in the garden," Felicia added.

Angie floured the counter and then took the mixed dough out to finish mixing and rolling out for pie crust. "Go ahead and bring them in now. I'll cut some for a fruit salad for lunch. I'm really loving having the garden here and so many people to cook for."

"You do this every day at the County Seat." Felicia put the bowl full of sliced apples on the counter and poured lemon juice into the water to keep them from browning until Angie had time to finish the crust. "Well, every day we're open."

"No, we do short order stuff. One meal at a time. Cooking for a large group is different. They have to eat what I make." Angie rolled out the dough. "I want to spend some time with Randy today too."

Ian came into the room with the plates from Randy's breakfast. "I have a lead on his son."

"You do?" Angie's heartbeat sped up. Getting Randy and his kid together would be the best thing to come out of the trip to the veteran's home. At least someone would appreciate their involvement. Carol didn't even want them there. "What did you find out?"

"Actually, it's a hunch, not so much a lead. Randy said that Mai's folks ran a restaurant in Nampa when Jacob met her. There's still a Vietnamese restaurant open in the downtown area. It's been there a while, but I'm not sure it's the right one. How about we head out for a late lunch after you get the crew going? Maybe we can find someone to talk to who knows the couple."

Felicia was drying her hands. "I can handle serving lunch and cleanup."

"Sounds good. I'm assuming they don't open until eleven anyway. We can leave here as soon as I get lunch set up and we'll be back by three to start dinner. I'll make salads this morning." Angie frowned. She'd wanted to spend some time with Randy but this was a real lead, no matter what Ian thought.

"Can I help?" Ian glanced around the kitchen. "Or should I go paint for the rest of the morning?"

"Go help with the painting. We only have two more days after today and I want to get as much done as possible. I'm not sure Carol's going to let anyone else in to help." She glanced around the kitchen. "I'll start on one section of the shelving before I stop for lunch and salads. I should be done by tomorrow afternoon with the kitchen."

"With an attitude like that, Carol should be thankful we're even here. I can't believe how hard it's been to work with her." Felicia paused at the doorway. "Are you sure you'll be okay in here alone?"

"I'm fine. Besides, I have Dom." Angie glanced around the kitchen, looking for her dog. "Wait, where is he? Did someone take him outside again?"

Ian pointed toward the hallway. "He's right there."

Angie peered into the dark hallway. There in the middle of the walkway was Dom. He thumped his tail on the floor when he saw her looking at him.

"He's lying right past Randy's room. But he can also see you. I think even your dog knows there's something up here and wants to keep an eye out on you and Randy." Ian moved toward the back door to follow Felicia out. "I think you're safe."

Angie smiled at him. "I'm always safe. Just pop in now and then for a glass of water and make sure, okay?"

"I can do that." He paused at the door. "Just yell really loud if something goes down."

"Okay. Got it. Run fast and yell loud." Angie glanced at her notebook. "Maybe I should write that down."

"Fine, you can't fault me for caring." He paused before he went through the doorway. "Just stay safe."

"I will, I promise." Angie put the pie in the oven and started water to boil for the macaroni and eggs for the salads. She glanced up at the first section of cabinets and grabbed a step stool. "No time like the present, Nona always said."

She climbed up and opened the first cabinet. The bottom shelves were filled with dishes. The next row up had several polished wooden crates. She found a metal tag on one and brushed off the dust. Reading the name, she frowned. "Muffy?"

Checking the others, there were five in total, she realized they all had names on them. She read the name on the last box. "Rover."

She almost dropped the box when she realized what they were. Pet ashes. She took them out of the cabinet and set them on the counter. Then she went into the pantry and found a shelf way in the back with the larger cooking items. "Sorry guys, you don't belong in the kitchen."

Once that was done, she came back out of the pantry and caught Dom watching her. "Look, I'm not trying to be disrespectful, but they don't belong in the kitchen."

He laid his head on the floor between his paws and whined.

Angie wasn't sure if it was in agreement or fear she'd put him into a little box. Shaking her head, she focused on the job at hand. She washed her hands again, then went back up the steps to get the stuff off the top shelf. "This kitchen is getting scrubbed."

She took down several boxes. Opening one, she found a stack of letters. These were addressed to Mary Elizabeth Owens, Randy's late wife. Glancing around the kitchen, she opened one and read the first line. "Dear Mom..."

Chapter 6

"Why are we bringing this box with us?" Ian carried the box to the minivan.

Angie glanced around, hoping Carol was still eating and not watching them leave. "Keep it in front of you. I don't want her to see that we have it."

"Carol, you mean. You're stealing this from the house." Ian shook his head. "Uncle Allen is going to know I helped you so I guess I'll be in the next cell."

"It's not her property. Just get in the van and I'll explain." Angie climbed inside, then had Ian set the box on the seat between them. "I've been on edge since I realized what the box contains. They are letters from Randy's son to his mom. I bet she knew exactly where he was all along. This might just lead us to Jacob."

"Well, start reading. It's not a long drive to the restaurant." Ian started the van and pulled out of the driveway.

"I've got a plan. I'm going to read the newest ones first." She pulled her notebook and pen out of her tote. She quickly sorted the envelopes by postmark if she could read it. If she couldn't, she moved the envelope to the back, assuming it wasn't readable due to the age of the stamp. Then she started reading.

She'd gone through two letters before she found the first clue. "They live in Boise. Or did in 1995. She worked as a nurse at the hospital. He ran a construction crew. They built a house."

"Well, that might just give us what we need." He pulled onto the main highway. "I wish I had my computer. Does it say the name of the company?"

Angie studied the pictures that fell out of the envelope with the letter. School shots. A boy with dark hair and bright eyes grinned at the camera with a missing front tooth. The girl was shy, Angie could see it in her face, but the camera had caught a slight smile. "No, but maybe he told her before. They have two kids."

"Hold those out. Randy needs to see those." Ian smiled as she held up the pictures. "He's a grandfather and didn't even know it. I didn't know my grandfather and I wish I'd been able to meet him before he passed. Randy's meeting these kids. I'm going to make sure of that."

"He's only living in that home because he thought he was alone in the world." Angie scanned the next letter for clues.

Ian turned down the music. "That's not exactly true. He knew he had a son. He just couldn't get past his pride to tell him he was sorry before now."

"Even if it means you live in a room alone?" Angie shook her head. "I don't understand pride."

"Well, he took the first step, asking us to help. Now let's see if we can reunite this family."

The restaurant was in an area of downtown that hadn't been part of the renovation craze the town had gone through a few years back. The parking was on-street spots and Ian pulled into one close to the front door. Angie glanced at the old brick building that housed the restaurant and a pawn shop to the left. "Looks like we missed the lunch rush."

"I'm not sure they had a rush, today or any day since 1965." Ian exited the van and came around to open Angie's door. "You sure you want to eat here?"

"Some of the best places look like this." Angie smiled. "Just don't order anything raw. Or any seafood. We're too far away from the coast."

"Good hints." Ian took her arm and they walked into Jade Table. The décor was typical Chinese American restaurant in reds and golds. Asian was Asian back then, especially in small towns. The booths were covered with aging red leather and the tables were Formica. But the smell was heavenly. "My mouth is watering."

"Ginger, grilled veggies, sriracha, and lemongrass. I might have just found a new favorite." Angie glanced at the sign. "Where do you want to sit? The sign says to seat yourself."

"Over there near the front. That way I can watch the door." He put his hand on her back and led the way. "It's a habit I picked up from Uncle Allen. He always wants to see what's going on."

"He's a cop." Angie smiled at the young woman who came to greet them. She waited for her to drop off the menus and the water glasses. "I was wondering if you knew the owners of this place. They had a daughter named Mai. About twenty years ago, I guess."

"Sorry, my husband and I own the restaurant now. We kept the name to honor the former owners, but sometimes I wonder if we should have changed it. Business isn't great in this part of town." She leaned closer. "Wait! Are you Angie Turner from the County Seat? Ben and I love eating there."

"I am. I'm glad you enjoy it. Next time you're in, let me know and I'll bring you back to the chef table in the kitchen. You can see how we make the magic." Angie glanced at Ian.

"We'd love that." She held out her hand. "I'm Xandra Holmes. So why were you asking about the Nguyens? They're super nice people. They still live in the area. They have a house near Meridian."

"We're trying to find their daughter and son-in-law. His father lost touch with him years ago and now he wants to make amends." Ian took up the conversation.

Xandra pursed her lips thoughtfully. "I don't really know Mai. I think she lives in the valley. That's one of the reasons the Nguyens wanted to sell. They wanted to spend time with their grandchildren."

Ian pulled out a card. "If you would, could you call them and ask them to have Mai call me or Angie? I'll write both of our cells on the back. We'd appreciate it."

She took the card. "Okay, I can do that. So what are you thinking about for lunch?"

"Why don't you surprise us?" Angie held up the menu for her to take. "I'm excited to try your food."

Ian handed back his menu. "Can you bring us some hot tea as well?"

Xandra tucked the menu under her arm. "It won't be what you're used to getting in England. Oolong's softer."

"And I thought my accent had all but disappeared." He shrugged. "I'm not picky. I take my tea as it comes."

"We were just in London for a holiday. So my ear might be tuned to the accent." She laughed as the bell announced another customer. "You two have brought good luck. I never have much of a crowd after one. I'll get your food and tea right out."

As they waited for the tea to arrive, Ian pulled his notebook out of his jacket pocket. "Okay, so the Nguyens live near Meridian. I wonder if Uncle Allen could make some inquiries."

"It's worth a shot. I'm going to chat with Randy when we get back and see if he knows anything else about her family." She checked the tea. It was still not ready. "Do you think he'll want the letters? Why were they in the kitchen?"

"Maybe he asked Carol to move them out of his room. They could be a sore spot for him." Ian watched the new arrivals. It was a younger couple who were more interested in each other than the menus. He nodded toward the two in a booth near the back. "Young love."

Angie turned her head in time to see them curve into a kiss. "I don't think I was ever into PDA like that."

"I was. Especially when I was a teen. English girls are the best." He poured her a cup of tea. "Present company excepted and all that."

"Apology not accepted." She reached over and took his hand. "Thanks for playing Greg to my Daphne."

"All we're missing is our Scooby-Doo. Of course, Dom isn't really restaurant appropriate." He lifted her hand to his lips and kissed it. "Any time, I love investigating with you. Just don't tell Felicia. She thinks she and Estebe are Greg and Daphne."

"In her dreams." Angie met his gaze and remembered why she had fallen for Ian in the first place. His eyes, his smile, and yes, his accent all tied up in a very nice package.

"And here you are." Xandra set two empty plates in front of them, then started sitting other platters around the table. "I know, it's a lot, but Ben and I couldn't decide on what we wanted to show you. These are our favorites."

* * * *

After stuffing themselves at the restaurant, they headed back to the house. Angie curled into the seat and tried not to close her eyes. "I'm going to go talk to Randy first, then I'll start working on dinner for the team. What's your plan?"

"More painting. Estebe was going to start on the upper level as soon as he was done with lunch. I'm sure he'll need some help to finish off the front before the light disappears. We might be able to get all but the back done today." Ian turned off the highway and onto the country road that would take them to the veteran's home. "And I want to call the hospital and check on Kendrick."

"Good plan. We only have two more days here. We need to make sure it's safe to leave them here with Carol." Angie yawned, the sun coming through the window adding to the stuffed feeling she had from lunch making her crave a nap.

"There's nothing saying they aren't," Ian reminded her.

"Besides Dom. He scared someone away last night, I know it. And Randy was supposedly on his deathbed when we arrived, but he's actually stronger now. Then Kendrick winds up in the hospital." Angie shook her head. "There's something going on, we just don't know what. Yet."

"Old people have health issues," Ian reminded her. "But I agree, something's going on. Uncle Allen's looking into the last guy who lived here. Phil was healthy as a horse according to his girlfriend from the apartment complex—until he moved in here after breaking a hip. When he died, the girlfriend assumed she would get the life insurance, but apparently it went elsewhere. The agent wouldn't tell her when he changed the beneficiary or who it was."

"Can I have three guesses and the first two don't count? It's got to be Carol." Angie tapped her fingers on the dashboard. "Does Randy have an estate? Where is it going?"

Ian glanced over at her. "How would I know?"

"We need to ask him. And find out if he knows about Kendrick's estate." Angie nodded and whispered. "Follow the money. It's always about the money."

"If Carol had so much money, why wouldn't she fix the house?" Ian pulled into the driveway. "I think your Spidey sense is way off on this one."

"We'll see. Thanks for lunch." She leaned over and kissed him before they left the van. "See you soon."

"Yes, you will." He grinned and jumped out of the van. "But for the next few hours, I'm a master painter."

When she went into the house, she stopped at her room and tucked the box under her bed. Then she headed into the kitchen. Carol was there, standing in front of the cabinet that had a ton of fruits and vegetables that Felicia must have brought inside.

"Your garden's putting out some amazing produce." Angie picked up a cantaloupe and smelled the core. "This is ripe. I'm going to do melon cup for breakfast. You have quite the green thumb."

"Oh, my thumbs are black. My ex-fiancé was the one who planted the garden this year. He loved to work out there. I didn't get the attraction. I'd rather spend my free time reading. Look, I'm sorry I jumped at you earlier. I've just been so worried about Kendrick. I don't need to lose someone else." She closed her eyes but Angie had seen the pain in them. "Anyway, thanks for all you're doing."

"No problem. I did need to tell you that I moved the pet cemetery into the pantry. They didn't belong in the kitchen." Angie nodded toward the pantry door.

"Oh, my, I probably had forgotten I'd even put those there. They were Randy's pets. All five of them. He didn't like giving them up but he didn't have room for them. He hasn't talked about the ashes for years." Carol smiled. "Maybe he's learning you can't replace family and friendship totally with a dog. Even if they are amazing. Your dog seems to like spending time with Randy. He must know he's a dog person."

"They're very good at recognizing people who like animals." Angie glanced around the kitchen. Either the team had taken Dom out for a walk or if he was asleep somewhere. Angie figured she'd find him in Randy's room. "I was surprised you don't have a pet."

"I did, a long time ago. I had a cat. When he passed, I just couldn't bring myself to get another one." Carol smiled sadly. "Anyway, I need to be working on the paperwork. So many reports have to be filed, you wouldn't believe it."

"I'll come by when dinner's ready." Angie nodded to the apple pies sitting on the counter. "The pies turned out lovely."

"I can't wait." Carol hurried out of the kitchen and toward her office on the other side of the house. Her bedroom was that way as well.

Felicia came in the kitchen from the backyard with a colander of blackberries and with Dom. "There you are. How was lunch? Did you find our missing child?"

Angie leaned down to give Dom a hug, then answered Felicia. "Lunch was amazing. You have to try this place. And we didn't find him, but we have more leads."

"Well, it wasn't a total loss. Did I see you talking to Carol when I came up? What did the witch want now? Did she offer you a poison apple?" Felicia took the colander over to wash the berries in the sink.

"Actually, she was nice. And apologized for being horrible. So I guess we don't have to call her a witch anymore." Angie was looking at the vegetables and trying to come up with a recipe for dinner. "Her ex-fiancé planted the garden."

"Where did he go?"

"What?" Angie pulled her thoughts away from listing off the ingredients for a tomato pie and wondering if they had ricotta in the fridge.

"I knew you weren't listening. Her ex-fiancé? Where did he go?" Felicia repeated. "He had to be here in the spring to plant the garden."

Angie met her gaze. "She didn't say. And she didn't say why he left. I thought the 'ex' part kind of explained it."

"Unless he was the one hurting the residents." Felicia turned to face her. "We need to find out more about him."

Angie sighed. "Add one more item to the list of things we don't know."

Chapter 7

Angie knocked on Randy's door. She had a tray with tea and cookies in her hands. Dom stood at the door with her, waiting to be allowed inside. "Do you have some time to chat?"

"Let me see, my schedule is so busy. Of course, I have time. The question is do you? Carol says you all have a lot to get done in a short period of time." Randy reached out a hand and Dom walked over to see him. "It's been kind of quiet today without Kendrick around. He's usually in here talking my ear off about one thing or another. Although if he tells you he went to London during the war, that's a complete lie. He was kicked out of the Air Force just before the war started because of a heart condition. He showed them. They thought he wasn't strong enough to fight, but he's outlived a lot of boys that went over to 'Nam."

"I hope he comes back from the hospital before we leave." Angie pulled the table closer and poured the tea. "I didn't get a chance to talk with him. Did you hear what happened?"

"Reaction to a new medicine Doc Sawbones gave him. I think that guy uses us as guinea pigs for the new pharmaceuticals they sell him on. Carol said he's doing better and will be home tomorrow morning." Randy picked up a cookie and took a bite. "He sure loved meeting your friends. All of our visitors should be as lovely as your group is. And the girls. It's been a long time since I've heard girls giggling late at night. My sisters used to do that when we went to bed. They're all gone now."

"I hope we're not disturbing your rest. I could talk to them." Angie watched as Randy poured sugar into his tea. A lot of sugar.

"Doesn't bother me. I like waking up to that sound a whole lot better than when Carol had her man living with us. I didn't like the way he talked to her. And he looked at us like we were paychecks rather than people. I felt like I was that orphan boy in Oliver Twist." He laughed as he picked up the cup. "And I'm feeling a whole lot better now that he's gone. Now, I'm not saying he was messing with my food, but my stomach is much better now. You can make your own conclusions."

Angie thought of the rat poison she'd found in the pantry and shuddered, hoping her reaction didn't show. She didn't want to scare Randy. "So why did he leave?"

"Carol got smart and kicked him out. He wasn't a good man." He glanced at the door and lowered his voice. "She could do so much better. I think he was just here for a place to stay, but I'd never say that to her face. She works so hard."

"You like her." Angie tried to hide her surprise.

He blushed and tucked his head down. "Now, don't you go spreading rumors. There's no fool like an old fool, right. Anyway, Carol's going to be fine. At least she will be when I pass. I don't have much, my savings and a life insurance. Of course, if you find Jacob, I'll need to change that."

"Did you know they had kids?" Angie pulled out the pictures she'd had tucked in her jacket pocket. "He and Mai had at least two. A boy and a girl. Their names are on the back of the picture."

He studied the photos, turning them over and then back, a small smile on his lips. "The boy looks just like Jacob did at that age. Where did you find these?"

"There was a box with your late wife's letters in the kitchen. I suspect you must have brought them with you when you moved in." Along with the pet coffins, she added silently. "I take it you didn't look at the letters?"

Randy shook his head. "When Mary Elizabeth died, I fell into grief. I stayed there for years. Some people from the church came and boxed the house up when I sold it and I moved in here. They must have realized they were sentimental."

"There are several from Jacob to his mom. Maybe twenty. Do you want them? I have them in my room." Angie realized she couldn't say it was because she'd thought Carol might toss them, so instead she said, "I wanted to have time to study them for clues."

He looked up from the pictures he now held with a death grip. "Did you find anything?"

"Mai's folks ran a restaurant in Nampa, like you told Ian. We went there today for a late lunch." She didn't want to get him too excited, but she could see the interest dance in his eyes. "They'd sold the place to a really nice couple. She said she'd give the Nguyens my phone number and ask them to call me. I told her I was trying to reach Jacob. She said the in-laws lived in Meridian."

"I remember them. Mary Elizabeth dragged me to an engagement party they held at the restaurant. They were nice people, but I was so mad. I was rude to them." He reached down and petted Dom's head. "I really need to talk to Jacob. Do you think you'll find him before you leave?"

"If I don't, I'm not going to stop trying." Angie patted his hand. "You'll see Jacob again. Sooner than later, I hope."

He yawned and Angie took that as a clue to leave him alone. "Sorry, I'm just so tired all the time. I never slept through the night when I got back in country. Not for years. Mary Elizabeth used to try to get me to take sleeping pills, the ones you can buy over the counter. But I hate taking any pills. I only do it here so Carol doesn't get all up in my face about it."

"I'll bring the letters in as soon as I finish reading the last few for clues. Unless you don't want me to." She paused at the door. Dom had already laid down, blocking the doorway to get into the room. She might have just lost him to Randy. He obviously wanted to protect the older man.

"I'd love to see them. She used to write me when I was in Vietnam too. I'd love to catch up on my son's life." He lay down and pulled a cover over himself.

Dom looked at her and whined.

"It's okay buddy, you can stay here. Just come get me if you need to go out, okay?" Angie could swear that Dom knew exactly what she'd said as he laid his head down and closed his eyes.

Felicia was in the bedroom reading the letters when Angie came in. She didn't look up but spoke. "Hope and Bleak are getting dinner ready. These letters are so sweet. I don't think I've gotten a letter from anyone for years. Emails, yes, but not a real handwritten letter."

Angie sat on her bed and pulled out the last few envelopes she hadn't opened yet. "Look for anything that nails down where they live or work. We need to find Jacob. Randy is counting on us. He made Carol his heir before he decided to find Jacob. Those kids need a grandfather."

"Wow. That's a motive to actually get rid of him." She paused, setting down the letter. "Ian found a bottle of eye drops in Kendrick's room. The hospital is checking his blood work to see if he's been poisoned."

"I thought it was his heart. Randy thinks it's a reaction to a new medicine." Angie thought about how Dom hadn't wanted to let anyone in Randy's room. Had he scared away whomever had the eye drops and they'd gone to Kendrick's room instead? "I wonder who's named in Kendrick's will."

"Do you think she keeps the residents' wills on site?" Felicia whispered, glancing around the room.

"Where is Carol right now?" Angie glanced at her watch. Almost four. If the woman had planned to visit Kendrick, she would have to leave soon.

"In her office. Do you want to go offer her the last slice of apple pie? She seemed to enjoy it last night." Felicia curled up on the bed. "I need to get up to speed on these."

"I'll be right back. Dom's in Randy's room. Take him out if he asks, okay?" Angie stood and set the letters down gingerly on her bed.

"Dom knows I'm his employee." Felicia nodded toward the door. "Go get going. Maybe we can figure this out tonight and not have to sleep under the same roof as a killer."

"As an alleged killer." Angie smiled and headed out to the kitchen. She waved at Hope and Bleak as she made her way through the kitchen and to the hallway where Carol had her private quarters. An office, a bedroom, and a bath, all off a hallway with a sign on the wall with one word: *Private.*

She knocked on the door to the office; no answer. She poked her head in, but she didn't see anyone, just a pile of papers on the small desk. And all the chairs, except one, had piles of papers. Angie stepped inside and saw a real estate poster, a business card stapled to it. She read it aloud. "Let me know when you're ready to sell. I've got a ton of clients who would love this property."

She's selling? Angie peeked on the back of the card. Theresa Yard's name and smiling face was on the front. Angie studied the room. If she was going to actually search for something, she needed some time with Carol out of the house.

Shutting the door quietly, she moved back to the living room, where she peeked out the front windows. Carol's car wasn't in the driveway. She moved to the kitchen and leaned on the wall in the arched walk-through. "Hey, have either of you seen Carol?"

"She ran into town," Hope said, stirring a pot on the stove. "She wanted to visit the hospital. You just missed her."

Okay then, that was a great sign. The lords of chance were telling her she had an open window to do a quick search. Angie nodded. "Bleak, could you watch out the living room window and tell me if she's coming back before I get done what I need to do?"

Hope shook her head. "You shouldn't be sneaking into Carol's private area. It's not right."

"I know, but I found a flyer saying she might be looking at selling this place, and if she is I don't want our 'charity' work to be used for someone else's gain." Angie also wanted to find out if Kendrick's will listed Miss Carol as the beneficiary, but no need to mention that.

"Well, I guess that's a good reason." Hope frowned. "I bet that was a survey post we found down by the pond."

"The one that Matt got his fishing line wrapped around?" Bleak grinned at Angie. "Twice."

"Yeah. I knew that looked familiar. When my folks sold my grandfather's farm, they had to have it surveyed before they put it up for sale as the lines with the neighbor were in dispute. Has Mrs. Stewart just been using us to get the house ready to sell? Where would Randy and Kendrick go?" Fire spit through Hope's eyes as she thought about the two elderly residents. "That's not right."

"No, it's not. Anyway, Bleak, can you be my lookout?" Angie hoped the girl would agree the transgression was worth the sin.

"Sure." She grinned at Angie. "I haven't done anything like this since I moved in with River Vista's police chief and Maggie. I swear that guy knows what I'm going to say before I even think it. Especially if I'm trying to hide something."

"Like kissing Ty after prom?" Hope teased.

"La-la-la, I can't hear you." Bleak ran to the living room couch, where she planted herself backwards to watch the driveway. "Angie, you better get busy. I don't think she trusts us enough to leave us alone in the house for long."

As well she shouldn't. Angie made her way back to the office and started going through stacks. Medical records, bills, household lists, emails Carol had printed off. The stacks were all about running the home and the warnings she'd gotten from the state on fixing the place up. The pile on the chair was about the last resident, Phil, whom Randy had mentioned. The one who'd died in the house. And a notebook sat on the pile. Dates and meals and a note about some guy named Brett's whereabouts on each day.

Was Brett the ex-fiancé? And had Carol been trying to prove his guilt? Or his innocence? She pulled out her phone and took pictures of the notebook entries. Then she went to the file cabinet. If there were wills in this sea of paper, she'd have them put away, somewhere. Especially if she planned on cashing in after the guy's death.

Luckily, the file was in the top drawer. Carol had three files in the will section and a stack of blank wills also in the drop file.

Angie glanced through each will and found the listed heir. In each case, it was Carol. And the wills were all dated within the last few years. Angie leaned on the desk, breathing hard. What exactly had Hope brought them to? Was Carol some sort of medical black widow? Not marrying the men, but taking care of them for the sole purpose of inheriting whatever riches they had at the end?

And worse, was she hurrying things along? Angie needed to talk to Ian's uncle, Allen Brown. He was the River Vista police chief and he could tell her if she was just seeing unicorns when there were really only horses.

She snapped pictures of the three wills, then put them back and looked around the room. She thought it looked like she hadn't been there. She turned around and ran straight into a man who'd been watching her.

"Oh, excuse me." She tried to walk around him. but he moved in front of her. "I'm expected in the kitchen."

"Actually, everyone's outside putting out a fire near the garden. You and your dog are cramping my style. Maybe you should get in your vans and leave tonight like Carol suggested." He leaned close and touched her hair. "You smell like lavender. I do love a fresh floral on my girls."

"One problem with that. I'm not your girl." Angie knew who was standing in front of her. The framed picture of Brett had been in Carol's trash. She could see Dom coming up behind the man, his teeth bared. She decided to push her luck and guess at a few things. "My dog doesn't like you at all. You should leave now, Brett. Carol threw you out once. She shouldn't have to do it again."

"Leave Carol to me. There's no way I'm letting her get all that money when the next two guys croak. Besides, the girl's in love with me." His eyes hardened. "Most girls want me."

Dom growled behind him.

"One last chance, leave now. Or Dom will chase you out," Angie warned. Dom was over one hundred fifty pounds, or had been at his last vet checkup. She thought he could hold his own with Brett as long as the guy didn't have a gun or a knife on him.

He held up his hands and moved toward the side of the hallway. Dom watched and moved with him until the dog was standing in front of Angie, and Brett had a clear path to the doorway. Or it would have been a clear path. Now Carol stood there, a bag in her hands and anger on her face.

"I thought I told you never to come back." Carol advanced toward Brett. "You get your sorry butt out of my house."

"Our house. And *our* realtor wants to put it on the market. She has a buyer, sight unseen. And it's a good price. You just need to get the last two old coots out of here. I've been trying to help." Brett's tone changed and Angie could see why women fell for him. He had a silver tongue built for lying.

"You hurt Kendrick, didn't you?" Carol shook her head. "I didn't want to believe it. But you hurt Kendrick and you killed Phil. Just for money."

"Not just for money, for you. For us." He stared at her, then at Angie. "Now look what you did. We have a loose thread we need to snip off. Kendrick wasn't supposed to be the one in the hospital. Randy was my target, but the dog wouldn't let me in the room." He started toward Angie, and Dom stood, baring his teeth.

"Brett, stop. Leave her alone. And just leave. I won't call the cops if you go now and never come back." Carol's eyes brimmed with tears. "Please get out of my life."

"Actually, you don't have to call the cops, I've already done that for you and they're here." Ian stood behind Carol. He placed his hands on her shoulders, then moved her behind him as officers ran in with guns drawn and surrounded Brett.

Once they had him handcuffed, Dom let out a bark and turned to give Angie a sloppy kiss.

"I'm all right. Thanks for the assist there." She knelt and gave him a hug. "You're awesome."

"Stupid dog," Brett muttered.

Police Chief Allen Brown stared at him. "You have the right to remain silent. I suggest you follow that instruction. Brandon, read him his rights. Angie, are you all right?"

"I'm fine, but I'm confused. Why are you here?"

Bleak came around Ian. "I called him as soon as I saw that guy set the fire. Everyone ran outside to put it out and I knew something was going on. I had Allen on the phone when he came into the house through the side door. I put Allen on speaker phone and got as close to you as possible without being seen. After calling Dom to help, of course."

"Lucky I was out in the county doing a drive around today or it would have taken me twice as long to get here from the station." Chief Brown hugged Bleak. "You did right by calling me. Even if you weren't quite sure what was going on. You have good instincts. Maybe you should go into police work rather than hospitality when you go to college."

"You're just saying that to be nice." Bleak blushed but had a huge smile on her face.

Angie grinned at the newest member of the County Seat family. She had followed Angie's instructions, but broken them when she saw danger. And she'd improvised. "I'm proud of you. Thanks for saving me."

"I wouldn't have allowed him to hurt you," Carol said from the side of the hallway. "I'm tired of people getting hurt. Chief Brown? I think I have the evidence to allow you to convict Brett for murder. Along with several other crimes."

"I did it all for you. For us," Brett screamed as the officers dragged him out of the house. "We were supposed to be together forever."

"That would have been a very long time." Ian came to Angie and took her in his arms. "I'm glad Dom took care of my light work."

Angie laughed and relaxed into his arms. "I can't believe he thought he could get away with killing whoever he wanted. I'm sorry I was snooping, Carol, but I wanted to see if Kendrick had made you his heir."

Carol nodded. "He did. And so did Randy. I guess I thought I was helping, giving them a person to take care of. I should have realized that Brett was poisoning them."

"Do you mind coming into the station with us? I've got some questions that need clearing up." Ian's Uncle Allen took Carol's arm and started leading her out of the hallway.

"Wait, we need the proof." Carol picked up a tote bag that was sitting on a chair. Then she tucked all the papers and the notebook into the bag. She stopped and looked at Angie. "Will you stay with Randy until I get back?"

"He won't be left alone, I promise." Angie met Carol's gaze and the woman nodded.

She smiled. "I believe you."

Then Carol walked out of the house at Allen's side. The County Seat crew filed into the hallway.

"Let's go into the living room and sit. I'll tell you all about what happened there." Angie led the way and then explained the last few minutes to the people who meant the most to her. Her work family.

Chapter 8

The next morning, Angie made a special breakfast. Bacon, made-to-order omelets, muffins, hash browns, fruit bowls, and mimosas. The front door opened just as she was finishing with the fixings for the omelets.

"I'm here with the package," Ian called out.

Angie wiped her hands on a towel and went out to the living room.

Jacob and Mai Owens stood there looking around with not two but three children. Randy was going to be surprised. Angie stepped over and held out her hand. "Mr. Owens, I'm Angie Turner. Are you ready to talk to your father?"

He shook her hand, covering hers with his other hand. "We've been trying to make contact since Mom died. First, he wouldn't talk to anyone. Then he just disappeared. I've been so worried. I thought maybe he was drinking his pain away."

"No, he was here." Angie smiled at the woman, who was too pretty and had all three children cuddled next to her. They were all touching her. Her hand, her arm, her shoulder. The kids were scared. "Let's go talk to him and then I'll bring in your breakfast trays. Any requests for omelets?"

"Denver, please," the young girl called out and her mother smiled down at her.

"Denver will work for all of us. Thank you for making our breakfast. It's not often a chef of your caliber cooks for a family event." Mai put her hands on the kids and met her husband's gaze. "I'm ready when you are."

"Then let's go talk to Dad." He straightened his shoulders and girded his loins against the fight he thought was coming. Instead, he was going to be met with love and attention, something he'd probably thought his dad would never give him.

Angie loved it when people outshone others' expectations of them and were even cooler. Randy's son and family could have refused to be part of the old man's life after the pain he'd caused, but they'd been open to at least starting a dialogue. Angie hung back and let the group go inside the room. Dom was in there with Randy but when Jacob and Mai went in, Angie called him out.

"This is a family reunion, big guy." She patted his side and he followed her as she went back into the kitchen to cook.

As she finished fixing the details of breakfast, Angie pulled out the list of things that needed to be done. Carol needed to get new residents into the building now that she was probably losing Randy. And before that could happen, she needed to be cleared of the legal issues and the house needed fixing. She read out the next items on the lists. "We have one more day here. What are we going to do now?"

* * * *

After breakfast, Angie waited for the family to leave before going into Randy's room. He was sitting at the window, watching the world pass by, but Angie could see a weight had been lifted off the older man's shoulders. "Okay if I pull out these dirty dishes?"

"You do what you need to do. Don't mind an old man reminiscing." Randy greeted Dom as if he hadn't seen him forever. "I hear you were a brave boy yesterday."

Dom slapped his tail on the floor several times. Then he wandered the room.

"He was amazing. How did your visit go?"

He shook his head and Angie's heart sank. Maybe Jacob had told him it was too late to try?

"They have a mother-in-law suite that they are moving me into next week. I'm going to live with them. Even with all the trouble I caused, they forgave me." He blinked away tears. "But you didn't tell me how you found them."

"Ian got a call from the other grandfather. He told us where to find Jacob and Mai. He said it was only right to honor the elderly." She thought of the words that Ian had repeated to her, mostly because he'd not believed it himself. "Be good with the kids. I hate to see you back in one of these after being hardheaded about something else. Like the proper way to fry a chicken."

"Don't worry. I'll be on my best behavior. And when I'm not, I'll try. That's all I can do, right?"

She leaned over and kissed him on the cheek. "I'm so happy for you."

As she left the room, Ian took the stacked trays. "You did a good thing here."

"Your uncle would say I was meddling again."

He laughed and nodded. "I can't argue that. But you did a great job. I was busy finding the clues to put a family together and you were trying to convince everyone that someone had been murdered. Never an easy feat."

"Maybe not easy, but easier with you and my County Seat crew." She motioned toward the counter by the sink. "Set those down and I'll finish washing dishes. Then we need to run into town and buy enough food to fill these cupboards."

As Angie washed dishes she thought about the last few days. Another solid case solved by the Scooby-Doo crew. She loved her friends and family. And that was the way it should be.

Have A Deadly New Year

Chapter 1

Sunlight streamed into the oversized kitchen and sparkled on the marble floor. Angie Turner, owner of the County Seat, watched as Hope Anderson, County Seat's dishwasher—and soon-to-be newest chef, starting next summer—took in the over-the-top room. Angie had to admit, it felt a little intimidating for her as well. Her home kitchen was the size of this place's pantry. And she could have fit two of the County Seat kitchen in the opulent space. The rich *were* different. And once the party was over tonight, this would be their kitchen for a week.

Felicia Williams, Angie's partner, had set up this catering job with one of her old boarding school buddies. Not only were they getting paid, they got use of the cabin for a week after the event. Angie had all kinds of projects planned for her kitchen staff. She just wished all of her cooks had been able to attend. Nancy Gowan had her kids this week and had bowed out of the job. Which Angie understood. Nancy worked so much it wasn't easy for her to find quality time to spend with her kids. But it would have been nice.

"Who did you say owned this place? The Kardashians?" Hope bounced over to Felicia, who was sitting at the table planning out the setup of dinner service. "I can't believe you went to school with this guy. What are you? Wealthy?"

Felicia didn't look up from the notebook where she was writing. "My parents are. I'm not. And Cliff wasn't either until his band took off. Look, you can't go all starstruck when you meet people tonight. They're just normal everyday people who have a band."

"And live in places like this. My parents' house could fit in this kitchen." Hope held out her arms. Then she saw Felicia's glower. "Fine, I'll stop being such a peasant and ogling. What's the name of the band? Do I know them?"

"Probably not. They were really popular a few years ago." This time Felicia did look up and met Angie's gaze. She sighed. "Fine. Cliff's the lead singer for Postal Mutiny."

Hope's eyes widened even more, and she sank into a chair. "OMG. Cliff Henry? That Cliff? He's like a rock legend. I thought Postal Mutiny broke up?"

"They did. Now they're going to do another album. This dinner is to celebrate their signing the contract in the California studios on Monday. They'll leave here for L.A. first thing in the morning, and we'll have the house to ourselves for a week." Felicia looked around as they sat in stunned silence. "Come on, guys, don't tell me you're all starstruck."

Estebe looked up from his tablet. "I am not struck by the stars. I do not know this band."

"Well, I do." Matt Young sank into a chair by Felicia. "This is going to be an amazing way to kick off the new year. Well, actually, end this year, since they'll be gone by the time the new year arrives. Is this why you took away our cell phones in the van? So we can't take pictures?"

"Exactly. You'll get them back on Monday after everyone's left. Cliff doesn't mind if we say we were in his house or that we catered the dinner, but no announcing the address or pictures of the band." Felicia made eye contact with each of them. "This is important, guys, I gave Cliff my word that we'd be discreet."

"Then we'll honor that, right?" Angie went to stand next to Felicia. "Matt's right, this is an awesome way to end our year. I've been excited about how well the restaurant has been doing, so part of our brainstorming is going to be about monthly themes. We get a week to live in this house. Just don't break anything. My umbrella policy isn't that large."

"So no using Ming vases for football practice?" Matt grinned but pointed to Dom, who was sleeping in the corner of the kitchen on the bed Angie had brought with them. "What about him? Does he know the rules too?"

Angie worried about Dom's ability to be careful in the expensive rooms. But she had a plan to keep him away from the really delicate items and close by her side. Maybe they'd leave with the house unharmed. At least she hoped that was what would happen. "Keep an eye out for him, will you? And if he seems to be somewhere he shouldn't be, bring him back to the kitchen."

"We will watch out for Dom. He's one of us," Estebe said as he closed his tablet.

Dom lifted his head, huffed, and lay back down. Apparently, he agreed.

"Are we ready to start cooking? Dinner's at five thirty." Angie reviewed the menu for the evening. They were going all out for their guests. An opening salad, then a garden gazpacho soup. A caviar-topped scallop appetizer. Beef tenderloin in a Wellington preparation for the main course along with potato/turnip mash, and one of Felicia's chocolate-on-chocolate desserts.

Tomorrow they'd start to work on a winter menu plan for the County Seat. She wanted some new ideas to spark more complex dishes to serve to their customers. But today, they had customers to feed. She wanted to have a good showing on the dishes. One, for the sake of the County Seat, and two, to show Felicia's old schoolmate what an amazing woman she'd turned out to be. Angie had a few high school naysayers she'd like to show what kind of person she turned out to be. But maybe that was just her. "Then let's get going."

The serving staff that Felicia had hired from the local temp agency showed up at five fifteen. Felicia left her spot where she'd been watching the chocolate souffle in the oven. Angie hadn't seen her friend so wound up about a service. Maybe there was more to this Cliff guy than just an old friend. Maybe they'd dated. The staff started getting ready to serve. With three of them, the food would go out to the formal dining room quickly and in one fell swoop.

Felicia had just come in from setting up the dining room with the servers when Cliff Henry breezed through the door.

He glanced around the room, his gaze falling on Felicia. "There you are. I wanted to get here earlier to greet you, but Bailey and I went shopping. I forgot to pack a jacket. Can you believe it? One of our crew members loaned me his for the trip into town. It's terribly out of fashion, but as the saying goes, beggars can't be choosers."

"The jacket looks fine, Cliff. Man, it's good to see you. It's been too long." Felicia fell into the rock star's arms. "You always promise you're going to come in a day or two early or fly back late when you're playing a local venue. But it never comes to be. What happened this time?"

"I guess I stopped in early this time, poppet." He kissed her on the forehead. "Introduce me to your lovely friends."

Matt ran to the guy's side. He pumped his hand with a maniacal look. "I'm Matt Young, sir. Thank you for coming to the end of the earth for your getaway."

"That's what getaway means. If I'm here, no one will look for Cliff Henry, the rock star. I'm just Cliff, the guy with way too much money that lets this place sit empty too many days a year. All the locals know me and judge me on that character flaw. Like every other rich person who has a cabin up here." Cliff slapped Matt on the back. "I'm trying to live up to their expectations of me."

"You're always trying to live up to someone's expectations," Bailey mumbled, and Cliff shot her a look. She rolled her eyes but went back to staring at her manicure.

"Muffy thinks getting the band together is a bad idea. We're not exactly on friendly terms right now, but at least we're trying. And it's the music that's important, right?" He hugged Felicia, then addressed the rest of the group. "I can't believe this one owns her own restaurant. I mean, she was always smart. She helped me through Algebra II and Calculus. But really, she was known for being the best-looking girl at school. Captain of the cheerleading squad. Drill team. Didn't you win a few beauty pageants senor year?"

Felicia rolled her eyes. "Mother's idea. She wanted me to earn scholarships to make sure I felt obligated to go to Brown. Her alma mater. My dad was pushing for Harvard. When Boise State offered me a full ride to the culinary program, I grabbed it. They didn't talk to me for a year. Thanksgiving dinner that first trip home was brutal."

"Cliff, give your friend a break and stop calling me Muffy." Bailey stuck her finger into Cliff's stomach. She smiled at Felicia as she added to the discussion. "I think you should do what you want with your life. You only have one. And living here must be amazing."

Angie got the feeling that Bailey's words weren't totally aimed at Felicia's situation. She locked gazes with Felicia. "I'm glad you chose Boise State. I wouldn't have met you otherwise."

"And I wouldn't have this cool job where I get to meet Cliff Henry," Matt added. When everyone turned to him, he shrugged. "What? I have a personal motto that it's all about me."

"You're the leading man in your own play," Cliff agreed. "So many people don't get that about life. Or if they do, they think the rest of us are two-bit players and not important. I suppose you'll be doing New Year's resolutions during your week? Make sure they're about you and not what others think you should do."

The venom behind the words surprised Angie, but once he realized he'd shown more than what he'd expected, Cliff let a smile transform his face. And she was left wondering if she'd imagined the pain she'd caught from his statement.

"Anyway, I just wanted to check in. We'll have about thirty people here for dinner, then all but six of us will leave tonight for home. The band will fly out tomorrow to L.A. for some business and promotion stuff." He sighed. "That part I haven't missed. I love sitting alone or with Dane writing songs. And performing isn't bad. But the media? They're vultures."

"You'll just have to plaster on that pretty smile of yours and they'll be eating out of your hand." Bailey ran her hand up and down Cliff's arm.

He turned to her and smiled. It was clear to Angie that Bailey was the rock Cliff clung to. She and Ian had a different relationship. He was at her house this week, feeding Precious the goat and Mabel the black-and-white hen. He was also working on a plan for a greenhouse at her farmhouse. If she could grow her own veggies during the winter, she'd have a better feel for what she could buy for the restaurant. They were independent of each other. Bailey and Cliff seemed to be joined at the hip.

Reminding herself that all relationships were different, Angie pushed away the judging thoughts. "Well, at least you'll get a good last supper before you have to start the media tour. Food can sustain you, especially during times of stress."

Felicia beamed at her. "Angie's on point. And the menu tonight will be filled with power foods, so you all should be ready to fight off any attacks."

"Unless they're from within," Bailey muttered.

Cliff turned and stared hard at her, making Bailey drop her gaze. Maybe he was stronger than he looked. "Sounds like a terrific meal. Anyway, we've got to go hang out with the guys for a while. FYI, there are ski runs in all directions here. So all you have to do is slap on a pair of skis, and head out on a trail. The lodge has a shuttle that will drop you off at the end of the driveway."

Bailey pointed toward the road that couldn't be seen out the kitchen window. "Not at the end of the driveway, but where our road meets the highway. It's about a half-mile trek, so make sure you're dressed warmly."

"They'll be skiing, darling. How else would they dress?"

Bailey blushed, and Angie wondered about their relationship. Again. Everyone else was starstruck with this guy, and she wanted to know more about his relationship. Angie wondered why she was even thinking about this. What was wrong with her? Angie tried to defuse the situation. "I don't think anyone brought skis."

"No worries, I keep a supply in the equipment shed." Cliff walked over to the wall by the door and took off a set of keys. "There's also snowmobiles and snowshoes available."

"We shouldn't, I mean, we're here for a retreat, not to ski," Angie said, but then she saw the pained look in Matt's eyes. She took a deep breath. "Fine, we'll carve out some time for some skiing. But nobody break any bones. If you do, I'll refuse your work comp claim. And I mean that."

Estebe chuckled. "Like a good boss, you're always thinking about the business first."

"Honestly, I just don't want anyone to have to go to the hospital. It really messes with the vibe of the retreat." Angie took the key from Cliff. "I'm putting it back on the wall, but seriously, if anyone takes off, please just let someone know so we're not worried. I'd hate to have someone freeze to death because we didn't know where to look."

"Safety first. In winter sports or in the kitchen." Felicia snapped to attention and sent Angie a sharp salute.

"Funny girl." Angie hung the keys back. "Anyway, we need to get back to work."

"We didn't mean to keep you," Bailey said as she laid a hand on Cliff's arm. "Thank you for agreeing to come and cater. The local girl didn't seem interested in doing the event."

"Maybe she was busy." Cliff put his arm around her. "We've got things to do before tonight's dinner. Lots to discuss. Wish me luck tonight."

And with that, the couple spun around and headed out the door. When Angie knew they were outside of eavesdropping range, she turned and studied her team. "Did that seem strange to anyone but me?"

"Rock stars are strange. Alice Cooper slept with his snake," Matt added to the discussion as he started plating the salad course.

"That's an urban myth," Felicia challenged. Then she held up a hand. "Besides, Cliff is one of the most stable guys you'll find in or outside the music business."

Angie shook her head. "Even I've heard stories about the band. Postal Mutiny is thought to have broken up because of the arguments between Cliff and Dane."

"That's probably true. I know Cliff would have stood his ground, especially if he thought he was on the right side of the music." Felicia glanced up at the clock. "If we're going to be ready to serve at five thirty, don't you think we should get busy?"

They were just completing the first course plating when a woman dressed in a blazer, white shirt, and pressed jeans stepped into the kitchen.

Her long straight black hair was pulled back off her face, and she wore a pair of black-rimmed glasses. She held up her hands. "Sorry, guys, we're going to have to push service back to six. Dane and Suzie just got back from skiing and need a few minutes to get ready."

Angie groaned, on the inside. The salad would have to be remade, as there was no way it would hold for thirty minutes. "Are you sure?" She stepped to the woman. "I mean, we'll have to remake the first course if we push it back. Will they be ready at six? Or will we have to push it again?"

"Look." The woman looked at Angie's chest, trying to find a nametag. When she didn't find one, she sighed. "I'm sorry, what's your name?"

"Angie Turner. Head chef of the County Seat. We were hired to prepare a dinner that started at five thirty by Cliff Henry. So who exactly are you?" Angie narrowed her eyes as she took in the woman, who had to be some sort of admin or secretary or personal assistant. The aura of positional power seeped out all around her.

Surprise filled the woman's face. Angie wondered if anyone had ever talked back to her barking orders before.

She glanced at the clipboard before she answered. She put on a smile that was friendly and apologetic at the same time. "Sorry, I should have introduced myself before shouting orders. I apologize. I'm Carolyn Hughes, Mr. Pines's personal assistant. I guess you could say I'm the band's cat herder."

Ignoring the joke and the attempt to win her over with what Carolyn must perceive as charm, Angie glanced at the clock. "You're asking for the dinner to be pushed back to six? Will everyone be available to eat by then?"

"Yes. I'll have everyone in the room so you can serve exactly at six." Carolyn's head bobbed as she saw a solution to her issue.

"Good. We'll serve then. By the way, your serving staff will have to be available then for another hour, so please remember that when it's time to pay the temp agency," Angie reminded her.

"I don't personally pay the bills, but I'll send a note to the accounting department of the change of circumstances." She looked around the room, paused her scan at Felicia, then nodded. "I better go round up the cats then."

Angie stepped back to the counter and glanced at the plated salads Matt had already completed. "Let's trash those and start over."

"Will do, boss." He glanced at the servers who were gathered in a corner of the kitchen. "Anyone hungry?"

The three women all came and grabbed a plate, as did Hope. Angie took two over to where Felicia was sitting and placed them on the table in front of her friend. "Was I too direct?"

Felicia laughed and picked up her fork. "No, and thank God for that. Carolyn's notorious for switching plans at the last minute. I bet she had some menu changes on that clipboard that she'd intended to bring up, but with you crawling down her throat at the change of time, she thought better of pushing it."

"Well, then, I guess I did my job. I hate catering, just for this reason. Remember the lady in San Francisco who changed her menu on the birthday meal for fifty, three times? The last time I had to tell her I was going to charge her three times what I'd quoted just for the changes." Angie bit into the salad. She smiled, finished the bite, then called out. "Great dressing on this, Matt!"

"Thanks, boss." Matt beamed at the compliment.

Felicia glanced at the clock. "All we have to do is get through the next four hours. Then they'll be gone when we wake up tomorrow, and we can have our retreat."

Angie nodded, but her first thought was that four hours was a very, very long time. She hoped Felicia's prediction would be true and the time would fly by quickly. From the way the dinner had started, Angie didn't believe they'd be that lucky.

Chapter 2

The shouting started during the meat course. Angie and her crew had just sent out thirty perfectly cooked beef Wellingtons to the dining room. They were starting to plate dessert when the raised voices came through the walls.

Matt walked over to the doorway and peeked through to the dining room. He turned back with a grin. "And so it starts. We're witnessing history."

"We're witnessing two guys who can't get along." Felicia kept working on the dessert plating. "Cliff always complained about Dane's attitude. He didn't like Cliff's ideas or the way the band was set up. Basically, Dane hates everything. It's really hard to be around all of that negative energy day after day. There's no way the band is going to be able to stay together after this album. All I can say is that someone must need the touring money really bad."

Angie frowned at the door. "You think we'll get our fee for this, right? Shutting down the restaurant for a week really cut into our estimated income. This catering gig was supposed to keep us in the black this year."

"I made Carolyn write us a deposit check that covers our outlay and most of the staff time for the week. We'll be fine. We overbilled this event because of the short notice and the fact they want us out here." Felicia finished the last plate. "These look wonderful. I'm snapping a picture to use on our website."

She pulled out her phone and took several pictures.

Matt frowned at her. "Why can you have your camera and not me?"

"Because I know what I'm taking pictures of. And I'd rather not police your actions while we're here. You'll get it back tomorrow as soon as they're all out of here." Felicia reviewed her shots, then slipped the phone back into her pocket.

Angie looked at the clock. The servers were still hanging around, and it had grown dark outside. "Why don't you guys take off. It's supposed to snow tonight, and I don't want you to have to drive in bad road conditions. We can serve the last course."

A tall older woman looked at her teammates. When they all nodded, she spoke. "That's nice of you. I drove us up here, but it's thirty minutes to where we met up and we all live in the next town over. We have another thirty minutes or so to get home."

Angie frowned. "I thought they used a local temp service?"

"They did. Ketchum is where the office is located. The prices for rentals and houses are just too high for any of us with regular jobs to live here. Most of the 'help'"—she grinned as she made air quotes around the word—"live in Haley or Belleview."

"Even that's getting pricy. My boyfriend lives in Picabo with his family and works at the lodge," another woman added.

Felicia handed each woman a check. "I know that the temp service will pay you and they should tip, but we'd like to thank you for making our food look so amazing. Part of a great meal is great service."

Their eyes lit up as they tucked the checks into their pockets. Again, the older woman addressed Angie. "Are you sure we can't serve the last course?"

"Go home. Drive safe. We'll be fine." Angie nodded to the door. As the women left, Angie glanced at the clock. "We have ten minutes before we switch out the meat course with the dessert. Who's got some cards? We could play a hand or two?"

"I'm working on dishes. I love having a dishwasher, but it's so slow compared to ours at the restaurant." Hope turned from the sink where she was rinsing plates.

"Well, if not cards, who has an idea for tomorrow's retreat? I'd like to cook at least two or three new dishes each day." Angie slipped onto a chair at the table and opened her notebook. "I'm going to play with a mix of potato, turnip, and leek soup."

Estebe sat next to her. "I wondered if we could make a sweet potato and russet soup. I think we'd have to puree the sweet potato to get it to the right texture."

For the next ten minutes, they talked about potato soups. What they wanted to try, what they'd had good luck with. By the end, Angie had a list of five different versions on her page. "Then it's settled. Our first cooking session tomorrow will be on potato soups. Make sure you bring all your creativity. We want this dish to be a collaboration of all of us."

"Kind of like *Stone Soup*." Estebe nodded.

Angie turned to him. "That's a children's book. Don't tell me you read that as a child."

He smiled, and crinkles around his eyes showed his humor. "I have lots of young nieces and nephews. I read a lot of bedtime stories."

Angie stood and picked up three dishes. "Let's do it this way. Hope, you follow Estebe out without desserts. You'll pick up dirty plates, then we'll drop. Hope will go to the kitchen, drop the dirty ones into the sink, wash her hands, then pick up desserts. We'll run two rounds of this, and by the time Hope comes out with desserts the second time, we'll be done."

"Great plan." Matt picked up three desserts, and Hope waited at the doorway to the dining room. When they were all inside, Hope froze. Carolyn was the only one still sitting at the table. The room, except for her, was empty.

Angie stepped around Hope. "What happened?"

"Hurricane Dane did his thing," said Carolyn with a sigh. "Everyone who didn't have to stay left as soon as they started fighting. It's a typical Postal Mutiny dinner. Dane screams about some stupid thing. Cliff tries to placate him. Dane gets louder. I don't know why Steve thought this would work again. They almost killed each other the last time." She waved Estebe over with the desserts. "Bring a couple of those over here. I'm eating mine no matter what happened."

Angie waved the rest of the group back into the kitchen and set the desserts she carried on the table. "Will anyone be back for dessert?"

"Maybe Bailey and Suzie once they get the guys settled. I'd leave about five dishes out just in case, but the rest can be thrown away. Just like this tour is going to be." She stood and went to the serving station where there was a pot of coffee. She poured herself a cup. "I hate my job."

When they'd finally got all the dirty dishes back into the kitchen, Felicia waved them over to the table where they'd set the dessert. "Everyone sit, and let's eat a few of these. I'm not sure how well they'll pack up, but I'm going to try. By the end of the week, they'll be gone."

Hope picked up her fork and took a bite. "They seem so happy on television. They slap each other on the back and joke around. Why are they like this?"

"Television isn't real life." Matt's shoulders sagged. His hero worship of the band members had been tarnished a little as well. "I guess they're just people like us."

"All celebrities, politicians, and people with money are just that. People." Felicia glanced at the group. "Just because some of us grew up in big houses doesn't mean we don't make mistakes or get our feelings hurt. We do, just like everyone else."

"Well said, Felicia." Estebe nodded. He pointed his fork at her. "And I'm more interested in the woman who made this amazing dessert than the woman who grew up with a silver spoon in her hand."

"In her mouth," Angie corrected.

Estebe frowned, confused. "I'm sorry? What's in her mouth?"

"The silver spoon. That's the saying." When Estebe still looked confused, she waved it off. "Estebe's right. Who we are now is much more important than where we grew up, right?"

Felicia sent her a grateful smile. But Angie's warning bells were going off. She hoped her bad feeling was a false alarm and not about the fight tonight.

* * * *

The next morning, Angie was in the shower enjoying the multiple massage jets and seemingly unending hot water when she heard a knock at her door. She decided to ignore it and enjoy the shower for just a few more minutes. The knocking got harder, and she heard Felicia's voice calling her name. Regretfully, she turned off the shower and wrapped herself in one of the cotton terry cloth robes that had been hung in her closet. She towel-dried her hair and finger-combed it before going to open the door.

Felicia stood in front of the door, shaking. She had her phone up to her ear. "Just get here as soon as possible. He's unconscious."

Angie froze. "Matt? Estebe? Who is hurt?"

Felicia shook her head. "We think it's Dane. I've never met him, but he looks like the guy on the album cover, only older."

"What happened?" Angie glanced down at the robe. There was no way she was going downstairs in this. She pulled Felicia inside and closed the door. "Tell me inside so I can get dressed."

Angie grabbed her clothes and went into the bathroom to dress. "I can hear you, so go ahead."

"Okay, well, Estebe and I were the first ones up. We were in the kitchen talking about last night and how crazy everything was. Anyway, he was making coffee, so I went into the dining room to see what kind of mess we had to clean up, and he was sitting in a chair. I thought he was asleep, so I started cleaning up the dishes, and I saw it."

"I must have missed something. You saw what?" Angie came out of the bathroom, pulling her shirt down and over her head.

Felicia shook her head. "He had a drumstick sticking out of his chest. His eyes were closed. When I reached out to touch him, he was warm and had a heartbeat. But there was so much blood." She glanced out the window. Gentle snowflakes fell past it. "They need to get here quick or he won't make it."

"Where's Estebe? Still in the kitchen?" Angie pulled on her tennis shoes and moved toward the door. "Let's go back down and wait for the police."

Felicia nodded. "I must have screamed, because Estebe came running. He's with the guy now. He told me to call 9-1-1 and get you and the others down there."

He wanted us all together where we could watch out for each other. Smart idea. Angie nodded. "You go get Hope up, I'll wake up Matt."

It took less than ten minutes to get everyone gathered up and downstairs. Both Matt and Hope were already awake when they knocked on their doors. Estebe motioned them to the side of the dining room by the doorway to the kitchen.

"Don't come any closer. We don't want to mess up the scene." He made eye contact with Angie.

"Maybe we should go into the kitchen and wait." Angie read Estebe's unspoken message. Their group needed to stay together just in case whoever had done this to Dane was still around. "Let's block open this door so we can hear Estebe. Felicia, do you want to sit there? Hope, get her a cup of coffee."

As they moved into the kitchen, Angie went over and checked the lock on the back door. It was open, so she locked it. Then she saw the door to the front of the house. "Matt, can you move that highboy over in front of that door?"

Matt nodded and scooted the heavy piece of furniture over in front of the door, blocking the entrance. "This should keep anyone out, unless they have an automatic rifle."

"Then we'll all slip outside and hide in the woods until help comes." Angie smiled at Matt's surprised face. "Yep, I'm thinking ahead. Come get some coffee, and we'll wait for the police, thinking more positive thoughts."

Hope sat at the table, as far away from the blocked door as possible. She had her coffee cup in her shaking hands. Angie poured coffee, then grabbed muffins out of the cupboard and put them on a plate. "In case anyone's hungry."

"After seeing Dane, I don't think I'll eat for a week." Felicia shook her head. "It is Dane, right?"

Angie just nodded, knowing what Felicia was thinking.

"There's no way Cliff could have done this. You have to know that." Felicia shook her head. "No way. You met him. He's a sweet, sweet man."

"Who was in a fight with the guy the night before. A fight that was so bad, most of the guests left last night so they didn't have to hear it." Matt sipped his coffee. "Look, I like the guy too, but someone hurt this guy really bad. And your friend had the motive."

"It's not our job to find out who hurt Dane. We're here for a retreat, and as soon as these guys get out of the house today, we're having one." She made eye contact with Felicia. "As long as the police don't ask us to leave the crime scene."

"And if they do, we'll just rent a condo. This retreat is going to happen. Come hell or high water."

Hope glanced out the window. "I think it's going to be frozen water that gets us. I was watching the news in my room, and they're expecting a blizzard tonight."

"They always overestimate the amount of snow we're going to get." Matt took a muffin and pushed the rest toward Hope. "Don't worry about it. We have snowmobiles if we have to figure out a way out of here."

"Unless someone tampered with them. That's what the crazy killer does in all the movies. He takes out all the possible escape routes." Hope took a muffin and unwrapped it with shaking hands.

"Stop freaking yourself out." Angie rubbed her arms. "You're supposed to be the overly positive one."

Hope shrugged.

"Okay then, we just won't talk about it." Angie looked at her watch. If the servers from last night were right, it would take the police and ambulance about thirty minutes to get up here. With the snow storm, she didn't think they'd be breaking any speeding records.

"Okay, so what do we talk about besides the guy bleeding out in the dining room?" Hope took a bite of her muffin as she waited for an answer. When one didn't come, she nodded. "That's the point. There isn't anything else to talk about."

They all sat in the kitchen, listening for the ambulance or any sirens. When they finally came, Angie let out a long breath. "I'll go meet them at the front door. You guys stay here. Hope, will you make a fresh pot of coffee? I have a feeling it's going to be a long morning."

Chapter 3

The EMT guys were inside as soon as she opened the door. She pointed to the right. "He's in there."

The lead guy nodded, and they disappeared. Then a man in a tan police outfit with a large brimmed hat came in, knocking the snow off his boots as he stepped over the threshold. "Sheriff John Pearson, ma'am. Are you the Felicia Williams who made the call?"

Angie shook her head. "She's in the kitchen. I'm Angie Turner, Felicia's partner in the County Seat, a restaurant. We're here from River Vista. We catered last night's dinner."

"And why exactly did you stay overnight? Typically catering companies leave as soon as the food is delivered." He pulled out a pen and the same type of notebook that Ian's uncle used.

"Felicia is friends with Cliff Henry, the owner. He gave us use of the house for a week after we catered the dinner. It was part of our payment." Angie ran a hand through her hair. "Look, I'm not explaining things well. Why don't you come in and have some coffee. We're mostly in the kitchen. Cliff and Bailey haven't come downstairs yet. Actually, none of the others have come downstairs."

Sheriff Pearson pointed up the stairs. "Jake, you take Hank upstairs and bring everyone down to the living room. Stay away from the dining room. No need getting everyone all upset."

At that point the EMTs ran back past us in the foyer. Dane was strapped to a gurney and had an oxygen mask on. "We're taking him to St. Luke's. I'll get you an update as soon as possible."

"Thanks, Kevin." The sheriff slapped the guy on the back as he took off at a run following the gurney. He turned toward me. "Let's go get some of that coffee."

When they reached the kitchen, Estebe was there. He'd changed his shirt and washed his hands before he'd come back to be with the group. When Angie met his eyes, he shook his head, letting her know the guy might have been alive when they took him out of the house, but Estebe didn't hold much hope.

She noticed he stood by Felicia, his hand resting on her shoulder.

Angie turned to the new arrival. "Guys, this is Sheriff Pearson. Sheriff, this is my crew." She went around and introduced everyone. The sheriff shook hands with the group one by one as she walked over and poured him a cup of coffee. Setting it on the table near an empty spot, she motioned. "I guess you want to interview us? If we do it one at a time, we could go into the living room, or I saw an office off the hallway you could use."

He looked up at her in surprise. "That's nice of you. You sound like you've done this before."

Everyone around the table, besides Angie and the sheriff, laughed.

Now the look on his face turned to confusion. "Did I miss something? Or say something funny?"

"I have a reputation for sticking my nose into the local investigations in River Vista. Although"—she held up her hand—"I swear it's not my fault. Either I'm a suspect because we're the new guys, or someone from my group is the suspect. Honestly, we're all respectful, upfront people. No shady sides here."

"You're forgetting about Matt," Estebe deadpanned. "He's the shadiest of the shady."

"Am not. You're the one who has more money than God. Maybe not all of it comes from legal methods?" Matt shot back.

"Children, let's keep our joking to a minimum. You're going to give the sheriff the wrong idea about us." Angie tried to keep the mood light, but from the look on the sheriff's face, she might be too late. "Look, Sheriff Allen Brown from River Vista can vouch for us. Although, full disclosure, I date his nephew. But it's a really small town."

He sipped his coffee then nodded. "Okay then. I'll do the interviews in that small office you mentioned. Do you want to take me there? And who wants to be interviewed first?"

Hope shot up from her seat. "Me, take me. I hate waiting, and my active imagination is too willing to tell me about all the things that can go wrong with talking to the police. I'll go first and tell my story, then it's done."

He smiled at the younger woman. "That's a great plan. Let's go get this over with."

"Like a root canal," she said, her grin infectious. "I know the office. I can walk you there."

After they'd left, Angie filled her cup. "What a mess. This is supposed to be a relaxing week, not another murder investigation."

"They do tend to follow you around."

Angie's head popped up as she considered Estebe's words. "You forgot to say 'but it's not your fault.'"

"Because I do not believe that. I believe we bring into our lives the things we most need to learn. So what are you learning from this, Angie?" Estebe leaned back in his chair and watched her.

"I really don't think that's fair." Angie was about to explain why when Hope came running into the kitchen.

"Sheriff Pearson needs to talk to you."

"In the office?" Angie stood and started to leave, but Hope put a hand on her arm.

"He's not in the office. He's by the front door. He's leaving." Hope stared into Angie's eyes. "He's leaving us here."

"Calm down." Angie nodded to Estebe, who stood and took Hope's arm to lead her to the table. "I'll be right back as soon as I talk to the sheriff."

He was on the phone, but he told the person on the other line to hold for a minute. "Glad you're here. I need you to keep everyone here until I get back. There's a missing child just reported in, and with the weather, I don't want to delay the search. I need to get everything handled on that front, then I'll come back and finish these interviews."

Angie shook her head. "No. You can't. You don't understand."

He put on his hat, but he paused at the door. "You'll be okay. I'll be back in an hour or so, three max."

Angie dropped her voice. "What if someone tried to kill Dane? That means they're still here. In the house."

He laughed. "From what I know of this group, he probably fell on the stick as he passed out from drugs or alcohol or both. You're perfectly safe."

"Okay then, but you better be back in no more than three hours, or I'm going to be freaking out here." Angie gave him a supportive smile, but she didn't feel very supportive. How could he just leave them there, especially without a clear-cut decision on what really happened to Dane. She thought murder was probably the most likely, but she wasn't a trained investigator. Just someone with a good Spidey sense. One that Sheriff Pearson thought she must have gotten out of a cereal box.

Men were infuriating at times. But she had to give him credit, at least he was asking for her help and not just barking orders. He looked at her, really looked at her, then sighed. "I tell you what. I can't leave an officer up here, but I can leave a vehicle. It will look like you've got twenty-four seven protection detail. It's the best I can do for now."

Angie knew the sheriff was convinced that whatever had happened to Dane had been his own fault. She wasn't as sure. She thought of her kitchen crew, her friends, heck, her family. She met the sheriff's eyes. "We'll see you in a few hours."

Angie watched out the window as the emergency vehicles left, one by one. As promised, a single police car sat in the oversized driveway now. It wasn't much of a protection, especially if the killer was in the house. "Not killer, Angie," she whispered to herself. "Attacker."

"Who was attacked?"

The voice came from close behind her, and she spun to see Steve Pines standing there, looking out at the police car. "Why are the police here? Why wasn't I alerted?"

"The police went up and knocked on everyone's door. You all were supposed to be down here a while ago." Angie took in the man standing before her. Apparently, he'd taken the time to shower, dress in dark jeans and a sweater, and put gel in his salt-and-pepper hair. If she didn't know better, she'd guess that the guy was in his early forties, but she knew that Postal Mutiny's manager had to be in his sixties, just from the bands he'd previously managed.

"Oh, I just thought that was my wakeup call for the trip to the airport." He glanced at his watch. "We need to get going if we're going to be in L.A. by dinner."

"You can't leave."

He frowned at her, probably wondering who she was even to think of giving him orders. "I'm sorry, who are you again?"

"I'm the caterer." Angie grimaced, knowing how stupid that sounded. "Look, something has happened. Dane, well, he was rushed to the hospital, and the sheriff told me to tell everyone to stay here."

"Well, I'm sure Dane will be fine. He's a pro at this overdosing thing. He knows just how much to take to get the attention he wants. He'll just have to meet us in L.A. tomorrow when he's released." He visibly relaxed now that he thought he had the problem handled. He smiled at her. "Don't worry, I'll call the sheriff and explain things so you don't get in trouble. Do we have coffee available?"

He turned and walked away from her but froze in the dining room. His eyes widened at the sight of the blood pool on the floor. "What the hell happened in here?"

"I told you. Dane was hurt." She didn't want to tell him exactly how hurt the guy actually was, mostly because it wasn't her job. Besides, he wasn't listening anyway. "The sheriff thinks he fell on a drumstick."

"That's impossible. One, drumsticks aren't pointy enough to cause this type of damage. And two, it would have had to be sticking straight up out of the floor for him to fall that way. Stupid police. They never know anything." He glanced at the doorway from the dining room to the kitchen. "Is there a different way to get there besides traipsing through that blood? I really need coffee."

She led him the other way to the kitchen. The chatter of her group stopped as soon as Steve walked into the room. "Guys, this is Steve Pines, the band's manager."

He walked straight to the coffeepot and took a cup out of the cabinet. He poured the coffee, then took a large sip, leaning on the counter and looking at them. Finally, he shook his head. "I don't understand what happened to Dane. You all look fairly normal for chefs. And he wasn't that drunk last night."

"He was drunk enough to get in a fight with Cliff," Felicia reminded him. "A fight mean enough that most of the band and road crew left before dessert was served."

Steve shrugged. "That's just the way Postal Mutiny is. The boys fight. We disappear and give them some space, then the next day, everything's fine."

"Except three years ago the fights got so bad the band broke up," Matt added to the story.

"Yes, both Cliff and Dane needed some time apart. Some time honestly to realize they needed each other. You know they both had a solo project that totally tanked last year. That's why we were getting the band back together. They needed each other." He sipped his coffee. "You can't think that Cliff had anything to do with this. He's a lamb. He wouldn't hurt a fly."

"I agree with you. I don't think Cliff could do this," Felicia added.

The side door from the dining room opened, and Cliff walked into the kitchen. "What am I being blamed for now? Spilling the wine in the dining room? It's my house. Why would I want to trash it?"

Steve hurried to pour Cliff a cup of coffee. "Sit down. I need to tell you something."

Estebe stepped closer to Angie. "Maybe we should block off the dining room somehow? We've got several others who might think the blood is just wine as well."

"Wait, that's blood? Who cut themselves on my carpet?" Cliff sank into a chair, his head in his hands. "You know that's going to have to be replaced now."

"The sheriff should have taped off the room. Although with this group, I'm not sure it would have stopped them." Leaving telling Cliff to Steve, Angie started going through drawers and pulled out a roll of duct tape. Then she found a black marker and took out sheets of paper from the printer sitting at the kitchen desk station. "Take this and block off the doorway."

Hope stood and took the paper from Angie's hand. "I'll help. I need to be doing something."

When Angie came back to the table after Estebe and Hope left the kitchen, Cliff glared at her. "Now you're putting that tape on my walls? Do you know what it will do to the paint? I had that shade made up specifically for the house. I'll have to repaint the entire downstairs."

"Cliff, we've got bigger problems than the paint." Steve watched as Cliff took a sip of coffee. "Dane, well, Dane's..."

"Just tell me what Dane did now. And if it's bad enough that we're going to have to postpone the album. I knew he didn't want to start working on the songs now. He's so involved in that stupid tell-all book he's writing. I swear it's his way of rewriting history so he'll look like the good guy in our relationship."

"Cliff, Dane, well, he's..." Steve looked at Angie, his gaze begging her to take over the story.

She shot Steve a look of disgust, then knelt next to Cliff to meet his gaze. "They took Dane to the hospital. He's not doing well. He lost a lot of blood from the wound."

"Blood? You weren't kidding?" Cliff's eyes went to the door to the dining room. "You mean to tell me that's not wine? Dane's blood?"

Angie watched as he closed his eyes. He slapped one hand on the table, and a little coffee sloshed out of the cup. She could hear his calm but forced breathing. Angie sounded just like that when Felicia forced her to go to yoga classes. Like a freight train.

He opened his eyes and stared directly through her. "Tell me he's alive. I need to be able to make amends. To make up for everything I've done to him."

* * * *

Angie and Estebe took Dom outside to get away from the group. Seven of the band had stayed over—well, six now, with Dane in the hospital. But it could have been thirty for all the demands these people had. She'd told them that her crew would handle the kitchen duties, but if they wanted laundry or housekeeping or, more likely, bartending duties, they were on their own. Felicia was making up a breakfast casserole with Matt and Hope's help. They'd moved the dining room table into a second living room and set up a juice bar and coffee station. When Bailey had come into the kitchen looking for someone to unpack her suitcase so she could find clothes for the day, Angie had bit the girl's head off.

"I still can't believe she thought someone would go through all her luggage just to find a scarf she'd forgotten to hold back." Angie threw a ball out into the grass that was blanketed in a light snow. "I'm hoping the sheriff comes back and lets us all go just do I don't have to put up with seeing her confused face anymore."

"I do not believe anyone has ever talked to her with that tone in her life." Estebe picked up the wet ball where Dom had dropped it by his feet. Her dog was an equal opportunity sharer of his drool-soaked toys.

"I know, I should be more empathetic." Angie rubbed her shoulder, where she was most definitely getting a knot.

"I did not say that. We have princesses in our family as well. My brother's children believe that they are special. So when they come to visit from California, they get the full treatment. And, even though they are special, at least in my eyes, they learn that being special is more about having a positive attitude rather than being treated as better than others."

Angie studied her sous chef. She was pretty sure he came from money, but you'd never know it. He came to work and did his job. He was the first to volunteer to clean the grease trap or redesign a recipe. He liked what he did. Which was a good thing because it really wasn't about the money Angie paid him. "Well, all we can hope for is that they all will be out of here sooner rather than later."

Estebe looked up at the sky. "Sooner would be better; otherwise, they may not get out of here until the storm passes."

"What storm?"

Estebe pointed up to the darkening sky by the mountains. Just then, the wind picked up and started blowing snow their way. She didn't know if it was new snow or just pieces the wind had picked up, but it felt like the temperature had just dropped by ten degrees. Or more.

She glanced at her phone. Maybe she should call the sheriff and see when he was planning on coming back.

She picked up her phone and dialed. No one answered, but since her call failed, it didn't surprise her. She stared at Estebe. "I don't think our hosts are going anywhere. Not now."

Chapter 4

Cliff was chattering in the kitchen when they went back inside a few minutes later. "Oh, good, there you are. We need to stay together."

Angie pulled off her coat and glanced at Felicia. "Don't get worked up. It's just a snow storm. They happen all the time up here. We'll stay inside unless Dom needs out."

Cliff rubbed a hand over his face. The guy looked like he hadn't slept in a week. "No wonder the sheriff said he wouldn't be here for a while. The snow closed the roads in town. We're a little west of town, so we should be seeing the start of the storm soon."

"It's here." Angie confirmed Cliff's announcement. "So the sheriff called you and said he wasn't coming? Doesn't that mean you all can't leave?"

"Not until we are questioned. He says that will probably be tomorrow or maybe even later." He shook his head. "Steve's going to throw a fit. He's going to have to cancel a bunch of appearances."

"Well, you can't schedule around a blizzard." And an attempted murder, she wanted to say, but she held back the addition. "How many of you guys are left? I brought a lot of food, but not enough to feed thirty for a week."

"Seven. Me and Bailey, Steve and Carolyn, Robbie, Suzie, and well, there's really six since Dane is at the hospital." Cliff went over and poured himself a cup of coffee. "The kitchen should be pretty well stocked. I ask the housekeeper to keep it set up, just in case we decide to come up for a getaway."

"We'll check the pantry then." She fixed Cliff with a hard stare. "Just to be clear, we're only doing meals. No short order cook will be available. We'll do breakfast or brunch around nine, lunch at noonish, and then dinner at six. But nothing fancy unless you happen to like what we're testing out for the restaurant. And we don't clean. We'll keep the kitchen clean, but the rest, everyone's on their own. And, you're going to get another bill for our cooking services as soon as we get home."

Cliff snorted. "I don't think Bailey's done her own laundry in her life. It should be an interesting experiment."

"Maybe we'll get out of here sooner rather than later." Angie met Felicia's then Estebe's gaze, offering them time to chime in, in case she'd forgotten something, but neither did. "Let your folks know if they're hungry, we'll cook now. Otherwise, we'll have lunch ready at two."

"I'll probably be the only one up earlier than noon. Well, besides Steve. Carolyn needs her beauty sleep." He stood and refilled his cup. "I'm going to go lay down the law with the group. Let me know if they give you any grief."

"We can take care of ourselves," Angie corrected him.

"No doubt in the world, but I'd rather you not have to deal with our misbehavior. We can be a spoiled bunch." He picked up his coffee and left.

"The rules are set. How bad can this be?" Angie looked at Felicia and then at the others. No one said anything.

Angie had planned on doing a day of the retreat on soups. The group had been staring out the window into the falling snow when she finished talking to Cliff. She studied the heavy snow, then brought her focus back to the group. "What are you guys waiting for? Did everyone bring a notebook? Let's see what we have to work with. I want a day of soups. One different idea out of each of you. And you have to use a primary ingredient that's available now. Locally."

"Like snow?" Hope pointed to the deck, where the white now covered the redwood stain.

"Like potatoes, or turnips, or kale," Matt corrected her. "Although snow might be a good descriptor of the soup. Snow day chowder."

"You always want to fancy up the recipe names. What's wrong with potato soup?" Estebe grumbled as he moved toward the pantry. "Or sausage and leek stew?"

"It's just a list of ingredients, not a name. What if people were called Five-foot Blond Man rather than Tony?" Matt put his coffee cup on the counter.

"We'd know exactly who to expect when someone made a reservation." Estebe grinned and slapped Matt on the back as he joined him in the pantry. "Let's make this interesting. Best dish gets to send worse dish out in the snow to clean off that deck."

"You remember I won last week's bet, right? You still owe me money for the sandwich contest."

Estebe shook his head. "You didn't win. I did."

Felicia held back as the rest of the team crowded into the pantry looking for ideas and supplies. She glanced at the dining room door. "Look, I'm sorry I dragged everyone out here. Now Dane's been hurt and what was supposed to be an empty house where we could work undisturbed is filled with people. I wouldn't doubt it if they all expect meals like last night."

"We spoiled them last night. What can you expect?" Angie gave her friend a quick hug. "I'm not letting this change up our trip. We're here to work and retreat and figure out the winter menu. We're going to do that. Even if they disturb us every hour on the hour."

"You don't know how pushy these people can be. Cliff's nice, but he's as needy as the rest of them." Felicia slapped Angie on the arm. "Stop grinning at me. So yeah, I used to be a spoiled brat, just like these people. Which is why I know this is going to be a disaster."

"Negative energy never produces a positive outlook." Angie hugged her friend. "Relax, it's all going to be okay. Besides, they seem like nice people. And you haven't seen the bill I'm going to send when this is over. The more we get annoyed, the higher our service cost will be."

"How would you know? We've only met half of them. We should have insisted on meeting people before we take private jobs."

Angie raised her eyebrows. "Why? Just in case we get snowed in again? Maybe we should just make sure we don't do retreats in the middle of winter. Let's schedule the next one in June on the Oregon Coast."

"Sun, sand, and with my luck, a typhoon." Felicia picked up her notebook. "I guess you expect me to play this create-a-recipe game too, right?"

"Of course. I can't be the only one playing the game with the staff. They'll gang up on me. It will be interesting to see what they create with limited supplies." Angie picked up her notebook and walked toward the pantry. "But you know we're going with my soup, no matter what."

"In your dreams, sister. We all have a vote. This isn't a monarchy." Felicia teased her.

"It could be. Queen Angie. Not a bad idea."

"I think you'd have a revolt sooner or later. If you even remembered to act like a queen. You're more a man-of-the-people kind of gal." Felicia paused at the doorway and picked up something off the shelf. "Ooh, butternut squash."

"I already claimed that." Hope took the squash from Felicia's hand. "You snooze, you lose."

Estebe chuckled.

Felicia turned to him. "What are you laughing at, big guy?"

"Nothing I'd say aloud. I like our relationship." He walked by her, his basket filled with items. As he passed by, he gave her a quick kiss on the lips.

"I guess you got told." Angie grabbed a basket and started looking at what was left. Potatoes and leeks—but the potatoes weren't the large russets she was used to working with. Instead, they were heirloom potatoes. In different colors, different shapes. She could roast them with a few yellow onions, then puree them for the soup. The leeks she'd mix in the soup mixture after she'd wilted them a bit. It was basic, but if she truly concentrated on the ingredients and making them the star of the dish, the taste would be glorious.

She was waiting for her turn at the sink so she could wash off her veggies when Suzie came through the door. She stumbled and almost fell into the table. Estebe caught her and led her to the table. Angie could smell the alcohol on her from across the room.

Suzie lifted her head. "I need something to eat."

"We'll have lunch ready around two," Angie said, trying to stick to what she'd told Cliff, even though she could see the woman was hurting.

She broke into tears again. "Dane's gone and now I can't even get a freaking sandwich." She screamed out the last few words.

Estebe set a cup of coffee in front of her. "I will make you something. I think we had some leftovers from last night. We are cooking right now, so we can't stop and make something specific, but I'm sure I can get you something."

She looked up at him, grabbing his hand. "You'd do that for me? Even though Dane's not here to see it? To reward you?"

"People don't need to be rewarded for doing the right thing." Estebe stepped away, then pulled two dishes out of the fridge. "Here we are. I knew there were leftovers. Give me a minute, and I'll have a plate ready for you."

Suzie sipped the coffee Hope had poured for her. "I know what you're all thinking. That I was just a piece for him. That he didn't love me. But he did. That's why he didn't want to go out on the road again. He didn't want to have to leave me home. Although I told him I would go. He was afraid I'd start drinking again."

And he'd probably been right to worry. Angie took in the woman sitting and sipping coffee while Estebe waited on her hand and foot. One piece of bad news and the woman had broken. The police hadn't even been gone six hours and she was drunk. "We're making soups. You're welcome to eat here in the kitchen if you'd like."

Suzie rubbed her face. "Maybe I shouldn't be alone. Bailey's holed up with Cliff. They're probably having sex. That's Bailey's answer to everything. She slept with Dane one night just because I was out of town. I take one night for myself and she slips into my bed. What kind of friend does that?"

Felicia's shocked face almost made her giggle, but Angie was more worried about Hope listening to this. Even though she wasn't a child, the girl was pretty naïve. Estebe must have felt the same way because when he got her plate ready, he stood her up and aimed her toward the door. "Why don't we go into the living room where you can watch some television. I think that will help you keep your mind off Dane's condition. Go ahead, I'll follow you with the food."

After they left, Felicia broke into giggles. "I knew Cliff's life was different, but wow."

"At least Estebe got her out of here before she started talking about her and Dane's life together." Angie opened the oven and checked on her potatoes. She stuck a fork in one, but it was still hard. She closed the door and turned up the heat.

"I don't know. I thought she was fascinating. I would have enjoyed hearing more," Matt said as he chopped veggies.

"Perv." Hope threw a dishcloth at him. Then she touched her cheeks. "Is my face as red as it feels?"

"Yep. You look like a fire engine." Matt grinned at her. "Maybe you should go have a cold shower."

"Maybe you should shut up?" Hope shot back.

Estebe stepped back into the room. "What's going on? I can hear you guys down the hallway."

"Just blowing off some steam." Felicia walked over to him. "You are a sweet man."

He put an arm around her. "I feel bad for her. I know she must have loved him, and now he's at the hospital fighting for his life."

Angie's phone rang. She stepped out of the kitchen and into the hall to answer it. When she came back into the room, she looked at her crew. "Dane's not fighting anymore. They lost him. The sheriff wants to make sure we all stay put. He thinks he can get up here as soon as the snow plow goes through if the storm stops soon."

The kitchen was silent. Felicia came and sat at the table. "Angie, does the sheriff think Dane was murdered?"

Angie sat next to her, and the rest of the crew joined them at the table. She looked around at her staff. Her work family. A family that was now snowed in with someone who had committed murder. "Yes. So we need to be careful and not be alone. No one goes anywhere without one of our group with you."

"Not even to the bathroom?" Matt joked.

Angie looked at him. "Not even to the bathroom. Estebe, you and Matt need to bunk together, and I guess the three of us will have a slumber party. Who has the biggest room?"

"That would be me. I have a master suite." Felicia held up her hand. When Angie turned to look at her, she shrugged. "What? Cliff knows I don't like sharing a bathroom."

"Then it's a party at Felicia's." Angie glanced at the clock. "We need to act normal, like we don't know what's going on until the sheriff comes back and gets us out of here."

The door to the kitchen slammed open, and Cliff and Bailey ran into the room. Cliff looked at the people sitting at the table. He dropped down next to Felicia's chair and grabbed her arm. "Oh my God, can you believe it? The sheriff says Dane was murdered. What are we going to do?"

"So much for keeping a secret," Matt muttered.

Bailey stepped back from the table. "Wait, you all knew? Did one of you kill him?"

"No." Angie pointed to a couple of chairs at the end of the table. "Sheriff Pearson called us too. We didn't kill Dane. Did you?"

Cliff's eyes teared up. "I can't believe he's dead. He was such a kind soul."

"He was a piece of crap, Cliff. He made everything more difficult for you, just because he could." She went around the table, stopping at the fridge to grab a beer. She twisted off the top, then sat in one of the chairs, Noticing the others looking at her, she shrugged. "It's five o'clock somewhere, right? Besides, Suzie's passed out in the living room. She started doing shots as soon as they told her Dane was hurt. Who knows what she'll take when she finds out he's dead."

"No one is judging you," Cliff said as he walked over to sit next to his girlfriend.

Of course, Angie thought, he was totally wrong. She was judging Bailey and Suzie for their lack of control over their drinking habits. But she wasn't their babysitter. She just wanted to get her and her crew out of here in one piece. Sooner rather than later. And she bet a few others from her crew were thinking the same thing. This craziness was definitely not her circus or her monkeys.

"What where you two fighting about last night?" Angie asked, watching Cliff play with Bailey's hair, his thoughts distracted.

"The usual. The business around the music. We never fought about the music itself. But the tour and how many stops and who should come along with us. Even what cut we should demand of the record company. Dane never got the point that the record company didn't have a lot of options in the contract. He always wanted more money, more promotion. Then he'd compare us to the freaking Beatles and tell me Steve was scamming us." Cliff sank even deeper into his chair, now chewing on the end of a pen.

"Dane thought he knew everything. Dane was more like an abusive husband than a partner. Or even a friend." Bailey sipped her beer.

"We shouldn't talk about him this way. It's disrespectful." Cliff closed his eyes and turned his head toward the ceiling.

"No, what he was doing, writing that tell-all book about the band, that was disrespectful. The best thing about Dane being dead is that book will never be released now."

Angie watched as Cliff pulled Bailey to her feet. "Let's go swim for a while. I need to relax and get my mind settled."

As the couple walked out of the kitchen, Angie glanced around the table. "We stay with our plan. Let's get moved into our new sleeping arrangements, and then we'll do a soup testing."

Felicia stayed sitting. "Estebe and I will stay here and watch the food."

"I think it will be fine." Angie stopped, realizing what her friend was implying. "Oh, yeah, I guess that's a good idea."

Hope fell into step with her and Matt. "It's like we're in that movie. Locked in a house with a killer."

"*And Then There Were None*?" Angie asked as they moved toward the bedrooms upstairs.

Hope shook her head. "I was thinking about *The Shining*."

Chapter 5

After they got their stuff moved to the new sleeping arrangements, it was time for lunch. The other guests came in waves. First Cliff and Bailey, whose hair was still wet from their swim. Then Steve and Carolyn. And finally, when Angie was just about to pack up the food, Suzie and a dark-haired man walked into the room. They both looked like they were in a haze—whether it was grief or chemically induced, Angie couldn't tell.

Suzie sat at the table, and the man slumped in a chair next to her. Felicia listed the soup and sandwiches still available. Suzie made her choice quickly, then turned to him. "Robbie, what do you want to eat?"

"Nothing."

"You haven't eaten since last night. Dane would want you to eat." Suzie lowered her voice and rubbed his arm.

Robbie snorted. "Dane would rather I be the one dead on a slab in the morgue. He wouldn't care if I ever ate."

"That's not true. You guys were friends. I know you were."

He rolled his head around on his neck. Then he looked up at Felicia. "Just bring me something, sweetheart. I really don't care."

Angie saw Estebe's back stiffen at Robbie's overfamiliar tone and words, but he let it go. Angie took the bowls and plates to the table for the two, hoping the guy wouldn't notice Hope. She was young, fresh-faced, and perfect in the eyes of a certain type of older man. Another reason sticking together wasn't a bad idea. She'd never forgive herself if anything happened to the girl.

For someone who didn't care what he ate, Robbie wolfed down his soup and sandwich. Angie offered him more, and he took a second sandwich, then stood in front of the window looking out at the falling snow. Dom watched him from his bed, not growling, but not being the friendly dog Angie knew.

"I don't think I've ever seen so much snow. I haven't been up here in the winter before. We typically jammed and learned new material over the summer, then Steve would book our tours and we'd be off for eighteen to twenty-four months." He barked a laugh after finishing the food. "I guess he's going to have to find a new group to boss around."

"You don't think the band will honor the contract?" Angie was curious. Other bands had replaced a major player without losing their own identity.

He finally looked at her. Angie didn't think Robbie had really looked at anyone directly in the eye since they'd walked into the kitchen. "Cliff won't let Steve replace Dane. He's tried that game before. I don't know if the fact Dane's dead would change that equation. Cliff loved the guy."

Suzie started to cry then and stood and ran out of the kitchen. Robbie sighed and started to follow. He paused by Angie. "The girl's having a bad time. She loved the guy. More than he deserved."

Angie picked up the half-empty bowl and plate and brought them to the sink, where Hope took them out of her hands. "First meal done, one more today."

Estebe pointed to the window and the still-falling snow. "I think it might be a while before they can get us out."

"Way to look at the bad side," Felicia said.

He turned to her. "There's a good side here?"

* * * *

If lunch had been strained, dinner was worse. Cliff came to the kitchen and took food back to his bedroom for him and Bailey. Carolyn picked up food for her and Steve. And Suzie and Robbie came and ate in the kitchen with Angie and the crew. As they were cleaning up the dishes, she turned to Estebe. "I'd hoped the sheriff would come back before dark. How long can this storm last?"

"Days, weeks?" Estebe shook his head. "I tried to watch the news tonight in the living room, but the local channel was off the air. I did, however, have the opportunity to buy a set of ultra-sharp kitchen knives, just like the pros use."

That made Hope snort. "Maybe I should buy those. My folks say they're buying me my chef set for graduation, but maybe I shouldn't let them spend so much on knives."

"Let your folks help you celebrate. A good set of knives will last you years." He cut into his lasagna. "It's a good thing they're doing."

"I can't believe I'm going to be done with school in six months. By July, I'll be part of the County Seat kitchen team."

"Excuse me? You've been part of the team since we hired you. You're just going to be in a new job. Which I hope you'll love. I don't want to lose anyone, not right now." Angie surveyed the kitchen. "Since we're done eating and cleaning up, who wants to take Dom outside with me for a little walk?"

"I will go with you." Estebe moved toward the door where their coats were hung.

Felicia pulled out some popcorn. "I'm making popcorn; then we can all go into the home theater and watch a movie. Cliff's got a lot of recent releases cued up for viewing."

"Are you sure it's not being used?" Angie snapped Dom's leash on his collar.

Felicia nodded. "I asked everyone. Well, I invited them to come and watch with us, but they all said they had other plans."

"Like getting drunk and passing out," Hope added. When everyone looked at her, she shrugged. "It's better to call a pig a pig than put lipstick on it. I've kind of lost respect for people in the music industry this week."

"They've had a shock." Estebe stood waiting at the door. "People do strange things when grief hits. You should be more understanding."

Hope's face turned beet red as she nodded. "Sorry, you're right. I was being uncharitable."

"Accurate, though." Angie smiled at her. "We'll be right back. Don't chose a movie without us."

"You snooze, you lose." Matt grabbed a metal bucket and started layering sodas inside.

As they stepped out into the night, the cold made Angie take a sharp breath. She moved off the deck and onto the path that Matt had shoveled earlier that day. The cement already had another inch or so of snow.

The snow was gently falling. Not as heavy as before. She glanced up into the sky and saw a few twinkles of stars between the clouds. "The snow might be stopping soon."

"Which means the sheriff should be here tomorrow. Hopefully, we will be fine until he comes back." Estebe took Dom's leash from her and let the dog run ahead of them.

"Are you concerned?" Angie studied his face. Estebe had good senses when it came to trouble. She trusted his guidance here.

"These people, they are not like us. Not even Felicia's friend. They are spoiled and used to getting their own way. Even when we feed them high-end food, they grumble because it should be better. Because they expect more." He glanced back at the house with the glowing lights. "We would be crazy to not watch out for each other. Staying in the same rooms gives us power in numbers. We don't want to isolate ourselves and become easy prey."

"But if Dane was killed for a reason, why would someone kill again?"

Estebe took out a bag and cleaned up after Dom, handing Angie the leash. Then they started walking back to the house. Angie thought he'd forgotten the question, but then he paused as he threw the bag and its contents into a trash can outside by the deck stairs. "Some people find they enjoy the act. If this is so, I am worried for all of us tonight. We are like fish in a barrel being stuck here with the killer."

When they got back inside, they took their boots and coats off and followed the group into the movie theater. Felicia had been right. There were a lot of movies Angie hadn't seen yet. They settled on a modern Christmas classic with Matt being outvoted for a more action-packed, violent choice. Angie figured they all felt a little too vulnerable to go with Matt's pick.

He grabbed a bag of popcorn and sank down into one of the chairs. "You all don't know what you're missing."

At the end of the movie, Angie glanced over to where Matt was sitting. He wiped at his eyes with the back of his hand. Yep, even her hardened chef had been sucked into the feel-good ending. She turned back to watch the ending when the door flew open and lights were turned on.

Cliff stood wild-eyed at the top of the room. "Bailey? Are you in here? Has anyone seen Bailey?"

Angie turned and stood up, meeting with Felicia as she hurried to Cliff's side. "She's not here with us. You both said you were going to turn in early."

"We did. But then I woke and couldn't find her. I've been all through the house. This doesn't make sense. Where is she?" He glanced around the room again, just in case.

"We'll find her. Let's go into the kitchen and start some coffee. Then we can make a plan to start a search." The movie credits were running on the large screen as they left the room. Estebe stopped and turned off the player as they made their way to the door.

She paused next to him. "What do you think?"

"There's no other entrance or exits from the room, so if she was here, we would have seen her." He shut the door. "We need to get the others up and in the kitchen."

"Why?"

He glanced down at her. "Because if she's been taken, the killer won't be where he's supposed to be. And if she's the killer, we need to be together. Not isolated. I'd rather it be just us, but we can't ignore his panic. He loves her and is worried."

"Which means he's probably not the killer." Angie watched as Felicia and Cliff reached the kitchen door.

Estebe put his hand on mine, and we waited in the hallway until everyone else had gone into the kitchen. "Or it means that not only is Cliff a gifted musician, he's an amazing actor."

Realization hit her fast as he watched for her reaction. "He did have motive. We've all heard him say that he and Dane fought about the project. Maybe Dane didn't want to sign the contract."

"Maybe." He took her arm, and they started walking again. "Either way, we need to watch him carefully until we're sure he's not the killer. It's a process of elimination, and this time, you have all of us to help you with your investigation."

Angie smiled at the tall, well-built and well-mannered man standing next to her. He wasn't a bad partner to have in a situation like this. "Sheriff Brown and Ian would say you're feeding my addiction."

"I'm just glad to have someone with your skill set here with me when I'm stuck in a snowed-in cabin with a killer. Otherwise, we'd all be just the next victim until help arrives tomorrow morning." Estebe held open the door to the kitchen, and they walked inside, ready to make their battle plans.

Chapter 6

"Okay, so our first plan is to get everyone down here and make sure Bailey's not with someone." Estebe took a notebook from the kitchen desk by the pantry. He moved it and a pen over to Cliff. "Draw us a floorplan of the house, level by level. And start with the bedrooms. We need to get the rest of the group down here sooner rather than later."

"She wouldn't do that to me. Not again." Cliff shoved back the notebook, glaring at Estebe.

"Dude, I think he meant talking to someone, not, well, you know." Matt took the pen and notebook and drew a box. "Let me help. I did some construction work during summers between college terms. I know how to work with plans."

Cliff took a deep breath. "Sorry, guys, I'm a little messed up right now. First Dane, now Bailey? What if something bad happened to her?"

"Let's just focus on finding her." Felicia set a cup of coffee in front of Cliff. Then she studied Matt's drawing. "So where are we in that box?"

"I think right here." He wrote *back* and *front* on the page. And then made a couple of lines in the middle of the line next to *back*. He pointed to one side of the kitchen. "So how many rooms are that way?"

"The breakfast nook, the solarium, then it drops down into another building where the pool and dressing rooms are located. You get there by going through the solarium." He watched as Matt added the rooms and adjusted the drawing a little to make room for the pool building. Then he pointed toward the front. "Dining room, formal living room, theater room in front of the solarium, then the housekeeper's quarters in the building in front of the pool area. It helps keep that private by blocking the pool from the road. On this other side are a couple of bathrooms, a recreation room, my den, and a music room."

"What's upstairs?" Angie couldn't believe how big the house was. Especially just the first floor.

"Bedrooms. And a laundry room. Same with the third floor. That's where my master is, and I put the others from the band up there so they wouldn't bother you." He didn't meet Angie's gaze when he said it, so she wondered if it had more to do with the fact that it would keep the help away from the band.

"How many bedrooms on each floor?" Matt asked.

"Four. No five. And a library on the third floor and a television room on the second."

Matt stared at him.

"No, that's all." He shifted in his chair when Matt didn't continue drawing.

Finally, Matt shook his head and muttered something about being different. Then he focused on the drawing and turned it over to Cliff.

Cliff studied it, then took up the pen. "It's great, but the library is here, overlooking the pool. It has a balcony. And the television room on level two is in the same place."

Angie picked up the notebook. "Okay then, this will be easy. We all go to the third floor and bring everyone down to the kitchen. We'll clear all the rooms on the third floor as we go. Maybe she's just reading in the library."

Cliff's eyes brightened. "I didn't think about that. I mean, I know Bailey can read, but she's never talked about reading a book or even a magazine. I have a couple of laptops up there too. She might be shopping."

If Bailey was shopping, Angie was going to be so ticked off. But she didn't think the girl was just sitting somewhere quiet. For some reason, she felt an urgency to find her. Glancing outside to the snow-covered deck, she watched the snow gently cover the path they'd made less than three hours ago. It had to be freezing out there. And if Bailey was outside in this weather, she didn't have much time. She stood. "Let's go find her."

They divided into two small groups of three. Estebe was with her and Hope. Felicia was with Matt and Cliff. When they got to the top of the stairs, Angie pointed to the left. "We'll go this way; you guys go that way. Let's meet here with the others before we go back downstairs. I like the safety of numbers."

"My suite is the one farthest to the end. You don't have to check that, I already did." Cliff pointed to the end of the hall.

"Good idea, let's start with the farthest room and work our way back." She glanced at Cliff. "Don't you want us to check just in case she went back to bed while you were gone?"

"Oh, good point." He looked almost hopeful.

Angie didn't think that would happen, but she thought anything was possible. And hope never killed anyone. Neither the emotion nor the girl standing next to her. She held out the flashlight she'd found in the kitchen drawer. Felicia had one for the other team. "Let's do this."

They made their way to the farthest door and opened it wide. The lights were on in the room and the bed mussed. Bailey hadn't returned. Angie made her way to the bathroom, where she found a walk-in shower she'd die for but no missing woman. Estebe stood in the doorway, watching the hall and the room at the same time. Hope emerged from the walk-in closet, her eyes wide.

"What's wrong?" Angie hurried over to her side, glancing in the closet.

Hope shook her head. "I can't believe how many clothes they brought for a week. They have suitcases full of stuff they haven't even opened yet. I guess that's their L.A. wardrobe? She has more clothes hanging up than I even own."

"But no Bailey, are you sure?"

Hope nodded. "No Bailey, but Angie, she has a real fur. I know it's real because I touched it. My grandma has a short mink, but this one, it's fluffy and new. And it doesn't smell like a dead animal like Granny's."

They walked through the rest of the suite, even checking out the large balcony. Angie leaned over and saw a hot tub set up outside near the pool house. A man and woman sat together with wineglasses in their hands. She tried to lean over, but all she could see was the woman's long dark hair. She pointed down, and Hope peered over too. "Someone's outside enjoying the heated tub."

"I can't tell if that's Bailey or not." She glanced over to the closet. "She has five suits unpacked in the chest of drawers."

"Let's hope that's her then." They went back inside, and Angie locked the sliding door to the balcony. "Did we check everywhere else?"

Hope scanned the room. "Yeah, I don't think there's anything else here where someone could hide."

They went out to the hall, and before going into the next room, which should be the library, she saw Estebe walking toward her. She met him halfway. "What's wrong?"

"Susie and Robbie are getting ready to come downstairs, but Steve and Carolyn aren't in their room."

Angie paused. "They share a room? That's a close working relationship."

"I didn't get that vibe either, but according to Cliff, they always share." He glanced down the hall. "Although I'm beginning to wonder if we can trust our host to be completely honest with us."

"That's a discussion to have with Felicia." Angie added, "There's a couple in the hot tub outside. It's probably them."

He nodded. "I'll go down and check. You all finish clearing the floor."

"You shouldn't go alone." She saw Matt come out of one of the rooms into the hallway. She waved him over. "Go downstairs with Estebe."

"But Felicia..." Estebe paused, then nodded. "I will trust you on this."

"What are we doing?" Matt asked as he followed Estebe down the stairs.

Hope was standing in the library doorway, watching her. "You don't think Bailey is in the hot tub with Steve, do you?"

Angie shook her head. "It doesn't seem likely. If Steve and Carolyn roomed together, then it's probably them. I think she might be more than just his assistant."

"She worships him. You can see it in her eyes when she looks at him." Hope stepped into the library, and Angie followed her. "I hope I'm never that gaga over a guy. I mean, I know love is amazing and all, but you have to focus on your life and what you need."

"You were raised in a different time than Carolyn." Angie thought maybe even she had been raised in a different time. Carolyn looked to be at least ten years older than Angie was, and that was being generous. Instead of saying this to Hope, Angie focused on what they were supposed to be doing. One wall of the room was covered with floor-to-ceiling bookshelves crammed with books. Maybe she could like this Cliff guy after all. As long as he wasn't just a hoarder. But Angie didn't think that was true. The library looked well-loved and used. A pair of recliners sat by the window under a reading lamp. A copy of a recent mystery sat at one table and on the other side, a copy of a regency romance. Who had been the reading couple? Cliff had already said Bailey didn't read. At least not around him. Somehow Angie found the mysterious couple so romantic. "Are there any doors in this room at all?"

"Besides the one we walked in through? Not a one." Hope spun around. "There's nowhere to hide or even take a nap where we wouldn't have already seen them."

"Nice room though," Angie commented as they made their way out to go through the next room. By the time they'd checked all their rooms, Cliff and Felicia were standing at the top of the stairs.

"We've already sent Robbie and Suzie down to the kitchen. Matt's meeting them. We're waiting on Steve and Carolyn to change before they join the group." Felicia glanced at Cliff. "I guess we repeat this on the second floor, then the basement, then main floor."

"And then we'll hit the pool and the machine shed." Cliff's tone seemed defeated. He was tired and worried, and those emotions showed in his entire body. "We should have started outside. She's probably freezing somewhere and we've just started searching."

"Cliff, calm down. We don't know where she is."

"She's probably gone." A woman's voice came from the doorway. Carolyn walked out in what Angie could only imagine was a lounging outfit. She'd call it sweats, but it was made of satin. "She probably killed Dane, then took off when she thought the coast was clear."

"Bailey didn't kill Dane." Cliff took a step toward the woman. "Take that back."

"You can't make me. She hated him. She hated the power he had over you. What was that power, Cliff? Why did you always back down when it came to Dane? What did he have on you?" Carolyn got up in the man's face, and Angie and Estebe stepped in between the two.

"You witch. You'd say anything. You never liked Bailey. You knew I wasn't going to fall for your games as long as she was around." Tears fell down his cheeks. "I swear, if you hurt her..."

"Look, things are getting a little heated here." Estebe took Cliff by the arm and moved him away from Carolyn and toward the stairs. "We need to calm down and think. Bailey could still need our help."

Cliff dropped his head and let Estebe lead him away.

"You are a complete chicken," she taunted him. "No wonder she left. She was probably tired of taking care of you," Carolyn called after him.

Angie saw him turn, but instead of anger in his eyes, she saw pain. Grief. Dismay. Cliff was starting to give up hope of ever finding Bailey, alive at least. She was about to say something when Steve walked into the hallway.

"My Lord. Carolyn, who are you screaming at and why?" Steve still had the towel and was drying his hair. He was dressed in an oversized Stanford sweatshirt and jeans. "What's going on? Cliff? Are you all right?"

"I will be. How do you even work with that woman? She's toxic," Cliff muttered.

Steve glared at Carolyn before coming over and putting his arm around Cliff's shoulders. "I'm sorry if she upset you. You know I need her expertise with the accounting. Let's put this spat behind us and focus on the matter at hand, finding Bailey."

"He's right." Felicia gave Steve a grateful smile. "This floor is cleared. We need to do the same with the rest of the house."

As they started walking downstairs, Estebe motioned Steve and Carolyn to continue their descent. "Please go wait in the kitchen with the others. We have a system developed for the search, and adding the two of you would just confuse the process."

Steve met Cliff's gaze, and when he nodded his assent, he put his arm around Carolyn. He paused as he realized Estebe was following them. "I know where the kitchen is."

"I'm sure you do, but I need to speak with my colleague for a minute." Estebe motioned downward with his arm. "After you."

"You can't think that we had anything to do with this," Carolyn started, but Steve put his hand on her arm.

"Let's go down and make some coffee. That way we can be helpful too." He smiled at her, and her shoulders dropped a bit.

Angie watched as they went downstairs. "I hope Matt can handle the four of them."

"They wouldn't hurt anyone." Cliff ran his hand through his hair. "I know how stupid that sounds, but I trust them."

"I hate to point out the obvious, but if one of them didn't do it, then you're on the hot seat." Felicia stood next to her friend. "I know none of my friends would kill Dane or hurt Bailey. You need to be thinking of why they were targeted."

"You don't think I have been asking myself that for hours?" Cliff nodded to the bedrooms. "Let's get this floor cleared. I can't stand the thought of her being outside in the cold and we're standing around talking."

The second-floor clearing went faster. And before they knew it, they were at the stairs again. Estebe quickly checked in with Matt, and when he came out of the kitchen, he nodded to Angie.

A lot can be communicated in just a head nod, Angie thought as they divided up the rest of the house. Mostly for her, the physical gesture was Estebe's confirmation that Matt was still in the kitchen and still safe. She hated the thought that he was in a room with a killer, but for all she knew, she might be working with one now. Just because Felicia trusted him didn't mean she did.

They finished clearing all the rooms and gathered in the breakfast nook, which to Angie looked just like the dining room, only without the blood stains. Angie sank into a chair. "I can't believe we haven't found her yet. Maybe we should check the cars. Could she have driven out of here?"

"No way. Bailey's a city girl. She doesn't even like driving to town in the summer. The roads are too narrow according to her." Cliff sat beside her. "But I guess we need to check the garage too. Three more areas to check. The pool house, the machine shed where the snowmobiles are kept, and the garage."

"There's six of us, let's divide into twos. Cliff and I will take the snow shed." Estebe gave orders like a four-star general. The good thing was when he talked, people tended to listen. It was probably his size that made them take notice, but it could be his demeanor too. He looked like someone who could make you do what he wanted. Good or bad. "Felicia and Hope, you take the pool."

Angie watched as he figured out his mistake. There were only five of them.

Estebe took it in stride. "Angie, you go with the women, and we'll not only clear the snow shed but also the garage."

"Or I could do the pool by myself since it's attached to the house, and Felicia and Hope can clear the garage," Angie countered.

"You shouldn't be alone. Matt..."

She cut him off. "Matt's watching the suspects. He's got a dangerous enough job without asking him to go with me just because I'm a girl."

"Well, it's not just that. You get into trouble when you're alone," Estebe admitted.

Angie shook her head. "That was not my fault. Not my circus, not my monkeys. And yet you're all looking at me like I'm damaged goods."

"We are not looking at you that way." Felicia sighed. "Okay, let's do Angie's plan. But if there's an axe-wielding psycho waiting in the pool for you when you get there, don't say I didn't warn you."

"That only happens in cheap horror flicks." Angie laughed as they headed to the pool door. The deck also had stairs leading down to the ground and to the garage and the storage shed. Several parkas were hung on hooks just inside the door as well as snow boots.

"Can't guarantee I'll have everyone's size, but there's a good selection." Cliff went to a drawer and pulled out a pair of boots. He handed them to Estebe. "Size thirteen?"

"Yes." Estebe looked down at his feet. "I can't believe you guessed or even had these. No one carries my size in stores. I have to special order them."

"Brothers from a different mother, dude. I recognize a kindred soul when I see one. Or when I see your feet, that is." Cliff slapped Estebe on the back. "There should be a couple of parkas in your size too."

"Well, you all go trudge through the snow. I'm heading into the pool area." Angie held up her phone. "You have yours, Felicia?"

"I do." She held it up and checked the power. "Fully charged. Be back here in ten minutes. No longer, or we'll all go looking for whoever is missing. And you better have a good reason for being late."

"Like being chased by an axe-wielding serial killer?" Angie joked.

Felicia met her gaze, her face serious. "Exactly like that."

Chapter 7

As Angie made her way to the pool door, she felt a cold nose touch her hand. She looked down to see Dom grinning at her. She stopped walking and leaned down to rub his head. "Who let you out of the kitchen?"

When he didn't answer, she wondered if she should go back inside and let Matt know she had him. She had ten minutes before Felicia would come looking for her. With the size of the pool area, it might take her that long to search the place by herself. She smiled down at her dog. Well, not by herself now. "Okay, boy, you can come sleuthing with me. Maybe this is what Sheriff Brown feels like when he finds out I've been investigating? You just stay out of trouble and don't be a hero."

He nodded his head happily. Angie figured the only words he'd understood had been that he could come with her. The dog was addicted to her company, she knew that. She just prayed that the serial killer joke had been just that. A joke.

She opened the door and felt the warm air flowing out at them. She'd expected to smell chorine, but instead, it was a floral fragrance that hovered around them as they stepped inside the pool area. They carefully took the several steps down to the pool deck, and Angie looked around. If she'd known it was this beautiful, she would have swum before she'd gotten ready for service. She'd make up for her bad decision just as soon as they found Bailey.

Dom watched as an automatic pool cleaner skimmed the top of the water. He took a step backward as he watched, then when it just kept coming closer, he let out two short warning barks and came over to Angie to sit on her feet, leaning up against her legs so she could protect him.

"It's okay, big guy. The pool cleaner isn't going to hurt you." She leaned over the edge and took in the Olympic-sized pool. Being rich sure didn't suck.

No body floated in the water. Neither had one sunk to the bottom. The clear pool water would have let her see a body, even if it was at the bottom of the diving area in the deepest water. The sparking water made her itch to touch it, so she knelt near the edge and touched the water. Surprisingly, the water was warm. Now she didn't envy Cliff's power bill. Of course, there were hot springs in the area. Maybe he'd been lucky enough to tap into one of those.

She was stalling and she knew it. She walked toward the dressing rooms to check them. Dom padded next to her. First room was filled with lockers and bins overflowing with clean towels and suits. Cliff took care of his guests. Bailey was nowhere in sight. Then she moved to the attached dressing rooms. Each one was totally separate from the others and had its own television. "People could watch movies in here."

She opened closets and bathroom doors, clearing one by one until she had gone through the entire row. Coming outside, she was now at the other end of the pool. "One building cleared," she told Dom.

She moved to the equipment room, which she assumed was filled with pool floats and other toys. Life jackets lined the walls. She covered every last inch of the booth. No Bailey. She left the side room and was just about to give up the search, when she saw what looked like a hidden hallway behind the equipment room. She turned the corner and found a door marked Staff Only. She jiggled the door handle, but it was locked. She turned to leave, when she heard a noise inside. Someone kicking something? "Bailey? Is that you?"

The noise sounded again. She got on her phone and called Felicia. "I think I found her. Come into the pool."

She hung up, not waiting for an answer, and tucked the phone into her back pocket. She studied the door. In the restaurant, they locked their cleaning supplies in a closet but kept the key close by so that staff could get in easily. Maybe she wasn't the only one who did that. She ran her hand around the door frame and touched a piece of metal. The key.

Angie brought the key down and gave Dom the command to sit. If there was just a rat or wild animal seeking warmth from the storm, she didn't want him to attack. She unlocked the door. The closet was pitch black. Again, she heard the noise. She reached over and flipped on the overhead light.

Bailey sat on the concrete floor, tied up with what appeared to be nautical rope. She stared at Angie, clearly not expecting to see her.

"It's okay, Bailey, you're safe. We found you." Angie moved into the closet and started to try to untie the knots. When she heard a noise behind her, she froze, hoping it was Felicia. Slowly, she turned and let out her breath.

Estebe grinned at her. "Leave it to you to win the scavenger hunt. Move out of there, and I'll get those ropes off her."

Angie squeezed Bailey's shoulder as she stood and moved out of the small closet. "Estebe will get you out."

"Bailey? Oh, Bailey, are you all right?" Cliff tried to squeeze into the closet as Angie was getting out. She grabbed his arm.

"Let Estebe get her out so we can see if she's hurt," she whispered.

Something in her tone must have gotten through the fear because he stepped back and nodded.

Angie watched from the doorway as Estebe took the gag off first. Bailey took in a deep breath, then started crying.

Estebe had his knife in hand to cut the ropes, but stopped moving and looked at her. "Are you hurt?"

She shook her head. "I'm just so happy you found me. I didn't think anyone would."

Estebe made short work of the ropes. Then he picked her up in his arms and carried her out to a pool lounger. When he checked her for injuries, Cliff stood back, holding Bailey's hand. Finally, Estebe stepped back and nodded at Cliff, who leaned down and hugged Bailey for a long time.

Angie and the other searchers stepped over to the supply closet. "She's not hurt?"

Estebe shook his head. "She has a head wound that needs cleaning. She probably was hit with something heavy to get her here. But why would someone go to the trouble to make her disappear?"

"Maybe they didn't have time to kill her and had her set up for when they had more time." Felicia pondered the question. "He must be strong to carry her this far. Maybe they thought they had killed her. If she was out from the head wound, the killer might have thought she was dead or close to it."

"If they didn't know any better." Angie glanced at the dolly next to the pool house. She walked over and saw blood spots on the metal. "This is how the killer got her down here. So we can't cross off the women from our list. Anyone could have gotten her down here. We need to find out where everyone was both on the night Dane was killed and last night. We should be able to narrow the attacker down. There's only so many people in this house. And with Bailey being attacked, I'm pretty sure the people who left are off the suspect pool."

"Yeah, that was stupid. If they'd just waited until the sheriff got back, there were tons of people in the house with possible motives. I heard one of the servers saying she'd slept with Dane the last time he was in town and he didn't even remember her name now." Felicia shook her head. "A woman scorned."

Angie stepped toward Cliff and Bailey, who seemed to be a bit stronger. "Let's get her to the kitchen and get some liquids in her."

"I could use a shot of tequila," Bailey said.

Angie smiled; the woman *was* feeling better. "Let's start with some water. I don't know how long you were tied up, but you might be dehydrated."

"It seemed like forever. Cliff had fallen asleep, but I was still awake. I got up to go to the bathroom, and when I came back to the room, I heard a noise. I turned toward the bed, thinking I'd woken up Cliff, and I felt the pain at the back of my head. Then nothing until I woke up in there." She glanced at the closet as they passed by. "It was weird. I thought I was dead."

When they got back to the kitchen, Matt greeted Dom first. He reached down and rubbed his ears. "There you are, boy. He slipped out on me, and I was worried he was off chewing up something really expensive."

Robbie laughed. "There's nothing really expensive in this entire place. Just a cabin in the woods."

Angie glanced at Felicia, who shrugged. She didn't know what Robbie was used to, but she thought everything was expensive. Especially the antique wooden furniture that Dom might like to use as a chew toy. She decided the barb was aimed at Cliff and ignored it. "Bailey, sit here. Hope, grab the first aid kit."

Hope pulled it out of a closet, but Estebe took it from her before she could give it to Angie.

"I'll take this. I've seen Angie's way of bandaging things." He took two clean washcloths out of the drawer and ran warm water over one, then added hand soap. "No one seems surprised to see Bailey returned to the fold."

"Why should we be?" Robbie muttered. "You went looking for her, you found her."

"Yeah, but I don't think the killer thought we'd find her alive," Angie added. She grabbed a notebook out of her tote she'd left in the kitchen. "Let's play a game."

"Let's not." Steve stood and finished his coffee. "I'm heading to my room. I have work to do."

"Actually, you're not." Cliff motioned back to the chair. Steve sat down. "I think Angie wants to ask us all some questions."

"What? Like she's some detective or something?" Suzie laughed. "You all watch too many movies. The guy who killed Dane is probably long gone by now."

"Then why would someone attack Bailey and leave her for dead?" Cliff stared at Suzie, and she sat back down.

"You think one of us is the killer." Her eyes widened as she looked around the room. "There's no way. I mean, a lot of people hated Dane, but this group, you were his friends."

"Friends that he was writing a less than favorable book about?" Cliff shook his head as Suzie blushed. "I know what he thought about me. He'd told me often enough that I was letting Bailey run my life. What he didn't know was how much I loved her."

Bailey smiled up at him as he took her hand. "I love you too."

"Fine. If that's settled, ask your questions." Carolyn stared at her nails. "Steve has work."

Angie wrote down everyone's name. "Okay, let's start with Saturday night. What happened after everyone left dinner?"

"Bailey and I went to our room," Cliff said.

Angie nodded, then looked at Bailey. "And you?"

"He just told you we went to our room." Bailey frowned. "Is this how you're supposed to do an investigation? Asking stupid questions?"

"You were up last night when he was sleeping. What were you doing on Saturday?" Angie stared her down.

"Fine. I went outside and had a smoke with Dane about ten thirty, once Cliff was asleep," Bailey admitted. "A smoke. I didn't kill the guy."

"You didn't say anything about that." Cliff squeezed her hand, then stepped away, leaning on the wall next to her.

"Because one, I know that you hate me smoking." She sighed. "And—"

"You wanted to convince him to leave your affair out of the book," Suzie interrupted, a gleam of pleasure in her look as she saw Bailey react. "Don't lie, I've already read all about it. You called me a friend when you were sleeping with my boyfriend."

"It was one time. A drunken mistake. I wouldn't call it an affair." She looked at Cliff, pleading in her gaze. "We were fighting about the last tour. I wanted to go home when we hit the US, but you insisted I stay with you. Dane was understanding one night."

"Sounds like he was very understanding." Cliff shook his head then went over and grabbed a chair from the desk and sat down. "So you were smoking, then you came back to bed. We know where Dane was at ten thirty. Anyone else see him that night?"

Steve nodded. "I must have come out just after Bailey left. Around eleven, I guess."

"Tell us about it," Angie prodded.

"I was down getting a glass of milk. My stomach seems to settle better with milk and this pill my doctor gave me. I saw Dane outside, so I put on a parka and went out to chat. I wanted to make sure he was going to be on board with the tour and the publicity. You know how he can get." Steve glanced at Cliff. "He told me he'd rein in his bad side. He said that he wanted one last chance to make music with you."

Angie watched the nonverbal exchange going on between Steve and Cliff. The guy knew just what to say to hit the heartstrings. Now whether or not it was true, that only Steve knew. "So then what did you do?"

"I went upstairs to bed. Carolyn was reading, so I put on my blindfold and went to sleep." He stood and refilled his coffee cup from the pot.

Angie turned to Carolyn. "So what were you doing?"

"Steve just told you, I was reading. Then a couple of hours later, I went to bed." She glanced nervously at Robbie.

"You're such a liar. I thought you didn't care who found out about us?" Robbie leaned back in his chair and studied Carolyn. "And I believed you. I feel so used."

Felicia kicked Angie under the table.

"Robbie, do you want to tell us where Carolyn was?" Angie turned toward the drummer.

He shrugged. "She was with me. I made sweet love to her all night long."

Suzie barked a laugh. "Probably more like twenty minutes, then you fell asleep, right?"

He squirmed in his chair. "Look, since I've gotten a little older, it takes some time. You have to be inventive."

"What time would you say you fell asleep?" Angie tripped over her words. She didn't want to start talking about his love life. She knew several appropriate responses would lead him right back to his memories and the wild sex he'd had. "And was Carolyn there when you woke up?"

"No, she has to go back to the man when the day breaks. I am only her night lover. Never in the light of day."

"This is just stupid. What do you care who I sleep with?" Carolyn's face was red.

"Let her talk, Carolyn," Steve said. His voice was calm, but it held a note of caution.

The room felt like it was a movie set and Angie was setting up for the final reveal scene. She met Felicia's gaze and could see her friend's concern. But she needed to press on. Angie turned back to Carolyn but focused on the paper. Like she was just following a trail. "What time did you leave Robbie's room?"

When Carolyn didn't answer right away, Angie looked up. The glare she got from the woman could have melted the ice in Angie's drink.

"I returned to my room at two a.m."

"Thanks." Angie wrote down the information then turned to Suzie. "What about you?"

"Let's see, I got in a fight with Dane at eleven thirty. Then I saw Carolyn leaving her room, and I followed her. She went into Robbie's room, just like she said. But she didn't leave at two. She left closer to midnight." Suzie stared at Carolyn.

"You don't know what you're talking about," Carolyn growled.

Suzie pointed at her watch. "I do know what I'm talking about, because I monitor my sleep. It shows that I was up from eleven thirty to twelve fifteen walking. I left Dane sitting in the living room watching the snow fall. I told him he needed to grow up and stop throwing these fits over nothing. Then I walked through the house several times. I like to get my steps in when he's occupied. I mean, I did. I guess I can walk anytime now."

"And that's when you saw Carolyn?" Angie pressed, not wanting the story to get lost in what she assumed would be tears now that grief was taking her over.

"I was at the end of the hall when she left Robbie's room. I guess she didn't see me." Suzie stared at the table. Angie wondered if Dane's absence was starting to feel real.

"Well, *you* have insurance on him. That's reason to murder him." Carolyn stood and pointed to Suzie, who was on the verge of breaking down.

"We all have insurance on our significant others. Steve insisted on it when we started the band. There's lots of bad things that can happen on tour. We wanted whoever we were with to be protected if something happened to us." Cliff stared at Carolyn. "But you knew that. Why are you attacking Suzie with it now?"

Steve turned to Carolyn. "Is there something you need to tell us?"

She shook her head. Then spun and turned to Bailey. "You were in his room looking for something last night. What did you take? Evidence of your affair?"

"She was not. You're throwing out red herrings to get the attention off you," Cliff shot back.

Bailey glanced at Cliff and took his hand. "Actually, she's right. I was in Dane and Suzie's room last night. I was looking for the tablet. I wanted to delete the section about our affair. I'd asked him not to write it. That it would hurt you. But he laughed and told me that we were way past a little thing like sex breaking us up."

"So did you delete the pages?" Angie felt like she was in a reunion show for some reality television series.

"No. I couldn't find his tablet. I searched, but it wasn't there." Bailey sighed. "And now you know anyway."

Cliff squeezed her hand.

Angie didn't think everyone caught the little gesture, but she thought that Dane might have been right. That they were past things like a little affair breaking them up. "I wonder what happened to the tablet?"

"I took it outside and beat it with a hammer until it was in pieces. That stupid book." Suzie sighed, sipping her coffee. "It consumed him."

"You crazy witch." Carolyn dove at Suzie, but Estebe caught her midair and pulled her back. She growled at Estebe. "Let me go. Do you know what that memoir would bring in a publishing deal? *I* helped him write most of it. I was entitled to some of the money when he got his advance."

"So you were going to just take it over after you killed him?" Angie took a chance that Carolyn was emotional enough that her question might just work.

"Of course I killed him. With him out of the picture, I'd take over. I could say anything. Anything to help the band." She turned to Steve. "Tell them. Tell them he was going to delete the manuscript. It wasn't fair. I deserved to be paid."

Chapter 8

Gasps filled the room. Steve just stared at Carolyn like she was an alien. "You killed Dane? And what about the attack on Bailey? Did you do that too?"

"You're not listening. I thought she had the tablet." Carolyn slowed down her words in her attempt to make her meaning clear to Steve. Her gaze was locked with his.

"Oh, Carolyn." He reached for her, then twisted her arms behind her back. "Does anyone have a towel or rope? We need to keep her still until the sheriff gets here."

Bailey raised her hand. "Hold on, I'll be right back."

Angie watched as the girl almost sprinted out of the room. "I guess she's feeling better."

When she returned she handed a pair of jewel-crusted handcuffs to Estebe, who was on the other side of Carolyn now holding one arm. "Here you go."

He held them up, his face showing his doubt.

"They're police issue. I have the key right here. I did the jewel work myself. They look rad, don't they?"

Estebe took the handcuffs, then led Carolyn to a chair. "They'll work then."

Angie crossed the kitchen to the counter. "It's almost seven. If the sheriff is coming, it should be soon."

Just then a door slammed in the front of the house. "Anyone here?"

Steve stepped to the door and called back. "We're in the kitchen."

When the sheriff walked into the room, he did a low whistle. Taking in the restrained Carolyn and the bandaged Bailey, he took out his notebook. "Well, I guess I've missed a few things. Fill me in on the details."

As Cliff took over the explanation using Angie's notebook to make sure he got the details right, Angie filled her coffee cup and watched. Steve sat close to Carolyn, his hand resting on her shoulder. Angie thought it was better that the book had been destroyed. Dane had been too scared to save it anywhere but the tablet. He hadn't even made a backup into the cloud just in case someone found it and leaked his secrets before he had the chance to get his payday. The book had ruined too many lives already.

Chapter 9

New Year's Eve, the five of them were huddled around a roaring fire in a large stone fireplace. The room was filled with overstuffed leather furniture and dark oak tables. Felicia had brought party hats and streamers for them. She sat with Estebe on the couch as Angie and Hope took the wing chairs nearer to the fire.

Matt crossed over from the buffet table with a plate of appetizers they'd spent the day making. He set them on the coffee table, then took the other side of the couch. "I never thought I'd say this since I was a fanboy about meeting the band, but I'm glad to be out of Cliff's house. Estebe, I can't believe you had a place here in Sun Valley and we didn't just have our retreat here."

"I didn't have a place in Sun Valley until yesterday." Estebe glanced around the dark wood-panel den. "And since the banks haven't opened yet, I don't officially own this place either. Please don't set it on fire or anything crazy, okay?"

"Wait, you bought this yesterday? When? We didn't get rescued from the murder house until noon." Matt took an eggroll and bit into it. "We came right here after the sheriff took crazy Carolyn out to the jail."

"I had been talking to a realtor since we scheduled this trip. I wanted to visit a few, but then I saw this one and the prior owners were desperate to get out of it. So desperate they were willing to sell it furnished and be agreeable to renting it out to me while the paper goes through." Estebe pushed a strand of hair away from Felicia's face and back behind her ear.

The motion was so tender, so intimate, Angie had to turn her head. "Well, this is a great place to spend the rest of the week. And it gets us out of Cliff's and Bailey's hair. Since they changed their mind about going to California for a few days, I didn't really want to push our agreement on them."

"Cliff says he'd send us a check for our time as well as our food costs. When I get that, I'll reimburse Estebe for the rent he had to pay along with some more for our retreat." Felicia squeezed his hand. "Thank you for rescuing us when we needed a place of refuge."

"Not a problem. I told you I'd been thinking about buying a place here. I'll rent it out for vacationers when I'm not here. It will pay for itself sooner than you think."

"How'd you become so smart with money?" Felicia beamed at him.

Hope raised her hand. "By the way, first thing in the morning, we're doing vision boards for the new year. It's kind of a family tradition."

"What is a vision board?" Estebe asked, looking warmly at the girl.

"You put all your hopes and dreams for the year into a picture by cutting out things from magazines and gluing them on the board. I brought all the stuff. It's going to be fun." She sipped her sparkling cider.

Angie's phone rang. The display showed it was Ian. She stood and went to stand in the hallway before answering. "Hey there, how's New Year's Eve with your uncle?"

"Quiet. Well, except for Bleak. She's got us playing Twister, and there's talk of some sort of Dance Party game torture coming after we celebrate the new year." He paused. "I miss you."

"I miss you too." Angie watched as Estebe opened a bottle of champagne and started pouring. "How's the zoo?"

"I hope you don't mind, but I've been staying at your place. The roads have been icy this week. Except tonight, I didn't want to drive back out to the farm so late. I'll go back tomorrow morning."

"That's fine. Give my regards to Allen and Maggie." She smiled and took the flute Felicia offered her.

"Tell Ian hi. It's almost midnight," Felicia said before heading back over to stand in front of the fire with the others.

"Tell her and the rest of your crew I said Happy New Year." He chuckled. "I just got a glass of sparkling cider. I take it you have the leaded stuff?"

"Of course. Want to stay on the line for the countdown?"

"Why do you think I called so late?"

Estebe started the countdown with the television program time-delayed from NYC. "Ten, nine..."

"Eight, seven," Angie joined in. She put the phone on speaker.

"Six, five," said Ian and the Brown family.

"Four, three, two, one. Happy New Year." The entire group cheered, and Angie smiled, feeling the love circling the room and coming through the phone line. She loved her life and had no regrets or wishes. Well maybe she had some wishes for the new year. She took the phone off speaker. "I love you, Ian McNeal."

"I love you too," came the response.

As she hung up the phone, she glanced outside at the gently falling snow. Tonight was perfect. Tomorrow may have its problems, but the present was just what she'd always wanted. Friends, family, a career she loved, and a place to call home. What more could she ask for?

Penned In

Chapter 1

Angie Turner closed the cooler that had held the salads and sandwiches the team had made for the outing. Their quarterly out of office meeting had turned into an adventure this time. With Matt Young doing the planning, they were sitting on picnic tables near the Boise Foothills and getting ready to be locked in the Old Idaho Penitentiary for the night. The good news was everyone had been able to arrange their schedules so they could participate. Of course, it helped that for their team building activities, The County Seat not only covered the out of pocket costs, but also paid an hourly wage. So basically, she'd be paying her staff to sleep this time.

She glanced around the table at her kitchen family. Matt was chatting up Hope Anderson who'd transitioned this summer from dishwasher to full-time prep cook. From the way the team was teasing her, Angie assumed Hope would always be considered the little sister. At least until they'd hired a new full-time dishwasher.

Estebe Blackstone, Felicia Williams, and Nancy Gowan were huddled around the other end of the table comparing notes on the new pumpkin salad that was in review to go onto the menu next month. And Ian McNeal, her boyfriend, was strolling back to the table with Dom, who had needed to be walked before they were locked into the jail grounds. According to the woman who'd set up their tour, Dom was welcome and they even had an inside courtyard where he could do his business. Provided Angie cleaned up after him, of course.

Dom was over a year old now and she thought he was still growing. He hadn't gained any height, but he looked like he'd been lifting weights lately. Having a Saint Bernard as a pet wasn't the easiest path, but Angie wouldn't change her decision for anything. She looked up as Ian paused next to her, letting Dom lay his head on her lap.

Ian gave her a quick kiss, then sat down, looping the leash over his arm. Dom laid on the grass next to the table keeping an eye on Angie's plate. "He was a good boy. Which meant I had to stop by the rest rooms and wash up afterwards. You could have gotten a toy terrier."

"Who wouldn't have been Dom. He's my sweet boy." Angie took a bite of the grilled chicken wrap they'd made up that morning. With the chopped peppers in the mix, the flavor profile was out of this world good. "Besides, I would have taken him. You didn't have to volunteer."

"I know. But I like helping. Especially since you let me crash the staff team building. I haven't even taken a tour of this place yet. I can't believe they're letting us stay the night. You do know that it's haunted, right?" He sipped his iced tea, watching her reaction.

"Of course, it is. Especially around Halloween, right?" Angie pointed over toward the Foothills. "And back there is a tree that moves from one side of the fence to the other when spooks are out and about."

Ian smiled and focused on his own plate. "I take it you're not a believer?"

"I don't know. I guess I've never seen anything otherworldly, so I choose to believe in the here and now."

Nancy sat down by her. "I have. I've seen a real, live ghost."

"Oxymoron, but okay, I'll bite. What's the story?" Angie turned to her chef and studied the typically serious Nancy.

A woman paused at the table. The woman's long brown hair was pulled back into a librarian bun. She was dressed in a guard uniform and as she squared her feet, she took in the table. Picking up a sandwich from the pile in the middle of the table, she sniffed it, then took a bite. "Good evening. I'm one of your jailers, Bridget Murphey. You can call me Officer Murphey. I hope you enjoyed your last meal because we're opening the doors soon and you won't be getting anything this fancy once you're inside."

"Are we staying near the haunted cells?" Matt raised his hand like he was in school. The officer glanced his way, then ignored his question.

"You'll have to leave your belongings in the lockers in the lobby area. Don't worry, we don't have thieves around, well, not in that part of the jail that is." She laughed at her own joke and took another bite of the sandwich. "You are permitted a camera, but not a cell phone. Which you should have been informed of when you were sentenced to attend this lockdown. You will be given a uniform shirt and a blanket for your comfort. The prison can get chilly at night. Some say it's because of the restless spirits in the building."

"I told you so." Matt crowed to Hope. She slapped his arm.

"Children, please." Angie turned back to Officer Murphey. "Can we bring in our cooler with sodas or will that be provided? I need to make sure I have water available for Dom."

"Your dog will be provided water from the tap. No fancy bottled water for any of you." She smiled down at Dom who slapped his tail against the table in greeting. "You may get a second blanket for him though. Any other questions?"

Matt raised his hand again. "Will we see all of the prison?"

"Your tour will include all of the safe areas. You will not be shown the cemetery. That is part of the botanical gardens." She glanced around at us one last time. "Any important questions?"

"Man, she doesn't like you." Estebe fake whispered to Matt. "Are you sure you're not acquainted with our new jailer?"

Angie saw Officer Murphey's mouth twitch but to her credit, she stayed in character. "Okay then. There will be four staff on site tonight. We're down from six, so you need to behave or you'll be sent to solitary on the first offense."

Matt looked like he was about to say something but the officer's glare stopped him.

"We have fourteen new residents joining us tonight, but just because your group is the largest sector of those, don't think you'll be getting any special treatment." She pointed to the stone front of the building and the large wooden doors. "Meet us there in thirty minutes without your picnic baskets. If you're not there, you'll be left outside and no one wants to be left outside alone on a night like this."

Since the weather was a balmy warm October Idaho evening, and they were in an upscale section of Boise where the nearby houses sold in the seven figures, Angie figured she was talking about the fact they were almost at Halloween. She waited until the woman began the act again with the small group at the next table before she turned to her group. "Ready for a haunted house tour? I think they're really going to play up the haunting angle tonight."

"I don't like ghosts." Hope said as she moved just a little closer to Matt.

"I do." Matt didn't notice her movement. He was taking pictures of the outside of the building. "Man, I hate giving up my cell. My camera on the phone is way better than this digital I have."

Estebe held up his camera with a set of lenses and a carrying case. "You need to buy a real camera, not rely on a device that does everything badly."

"My phone is the newest model. I bet the pictures I take kill yours." He snapped several pictures of the table, then of the outside of the prison. "I'm a master at this."

"Except for the fact that you can't take it inside the prison, I might take you up on that bet." Estebe patted his camera case. "I guess I'll have to share my pictures with the group so we can all have memories of this exciting outing. Thanks for setting it up."

Matt started to say something, then swallowed his words. He'd lost the battle, everyone at the table could see that. But if he moderated his response, he might come back harder another day to win the war.

Angie rolled her eyes at Ian who just laughed. "They're your children, not mine."

"And that's exactly what they are – children." She glanced around the table. "If everyone's finished eating, let's pack up the coolers. Put them in my vehicle and I'll stop at the shop and clean up in the morning."

"Hold it," Felicia called out. She pointed to the dark SUV at the end of the parking lot. "Just put everything into Estebe's Hummer. He has to drop me off at my apartment anyway so I might as well take care of the cleanup. That way Angie can just go straight home without coming into River Vista."

"You don't have to," Angie started but Felicia shook her head. After throwing away her paper plate, she walked over and stood next to Angie.

"I know I don't have to, but I am a full partner, right?" When Angie nodded, Felicia continued. "Then that means I clean up at times too. Besides, you'll probably need to hurry home to feed Precious and Mabel."

"Actually, Erica's coming from across the street for tonight and tomorrow morning's feedings, so I'm good. But I'll let you clean up. Especially since Estebe and I cooked."

With many hands, the dinner mess was cleaned up in no time. Ian stood next to her, looking at the prison. "It's formidable. Can you believe that most of it was built with prison labor? No construction crews here."

"They hauled a lot of rock in from the river for that front." Angie glanced at the other buildings. "Most of these are made out of rock. That's crazy."

"It kept the prisoners in. Although if I was incarcerated and forced to build my own jail, I might just build some secret escape hatch, just in case my parole didn't come through when I needed it." Ian pointed to the door that was opening. "Looks like the fun is beginning."

Four people in guard uniforms walked through the front door. They waved everyone closer. One of the guards was the young woman who'd come by their table earlier. The other three looked so much alike, Angie wondered if they were related.

Hope stood by her side. She glanced up at Angie with a small smile on her face. "I hope this isn't scary. I hate scary movies. I'd triple hate being in one."

Angie put one hand on Hope's shoulder and squeezed. "It's team building, not scream building. Relax, it's just a play. A theater of sorts. Everyone's just playing a role."

As they walked to the four guards who were motioning them inside, Hope sighed. "That's what I'm afraid of. I don't want to play a role in this crazy play. I just want to get out alive with my friends by my side."

Angie felt the change in temperature as soon as she walked through the doors. The stone walls kept the building cool, even in deep summer. Which tended to last for less than a week. Goosebumps prickled her arms.

"Isn't this the coolest?" Matt asked.

Hope shook her head. "This is crazy, that's what it is. I've got a bad feeling about this."

Hope looked like she was about to bolt. Angie met Estebe's gaze and he nodded, stepping closer to the young woman. "Just stay by me. Nothing is going to hurt you. I won't let it."

She smiled up at him. "That's kind of you, but I'm not afraid of real people."

He held up a St. Christopher's medal. "My mama told me as long as I wore this, nothing on earth or heaven or hell could get me. I have faith. I know you do as well, so let's just focus on our faith and have fun with our friends."

"In the lion's den." Hope shook her head. "You're right. I'm being a baby. Let's get this party started."

A male guard stood on a podium. "Go ahead and grab a locker. The keys are on lanyards so you can keep them close at hand. Just in case you need a quick getaway."

Another guard jumped up on the platform. "Just don't be thinking you're actually going to get out of here. You're ours until we release you in the morning. No whining, no back talk, and especially, no crying. I hate crybabies."

Hope's eyes widened as she stepped closer to Estebe. Even Matt swallowed a bit as he watched the guard slap a night stick in his hand.

"Visit a prison, it will be fun, they said," Felicia muttered loud enough for the group to hear. Angie smothered a laugh as the prison guard stared at their group.

"If the comedy act is done back there, let's get your belongings and valuables in a locker. Keep your key close by, you never know when you might have to leave unexpectedly. You can have cameras and a small notebook, but nothing else." He grinned but the action held no warmth or no humor.

"I'm beginning to think we stepped back in time." Angie said to Ian as she made her way to a locker. He put his wallet and phone in the same locker and took the one key. He tucked it into his shirt.

"We'll be fine. It's all an act." Ian put an arm around her waist. "Come with me and see my new digs, doll. I'll be home in five to ten."

"Not funny. I don't date convicts." She glanced back to make sure the others were close by.

"Then we may need to have a little talk when we get out of here." Ian stared into her eyes. "I've got a small confession."

Chapter 2

Angie stared at him. "What are you talking about?"

He shook his head and pointed to the guard. "Better we talk after we get out of here. I'd hate for that guy to think I was a serial offender. He might not take a liking to my melodious British accent."

"You're messing with me, right?" Angie tried to push the question, but Ian just stepped away and stood by Estebe. "Men. Go ahead and avoid the question."

Felicia stepped closer to Angie. She leaned close and whispered. "Are you two fighting? You never fight."

"We're not fighting." Angie started to tell Felicia what happened but then the lights went out.

A woman screamed behind them. Angie could hear rustling as people tried to find out who had screamed. The lights came back on and Angie saw Hope's bright red face.

"Sorry everyone, I overreacted. I'm fine." Hope called out to the crowd.

"Well, that's a relief," Bridget said but her tone seemed mocking. She let the group settle. "First we'll take a tour of the facility. We have a large gun collection in the gallows room. I think you'll be impressed. Then we'll do the general population quarters and finally, we'll take you to your cells. You can hang out there, or we'll be having coffee and dessert in the dining room at the end of the tour."

"See, Hope, nothing to worry about. We're just touring a building." Estebe patted her back like an inexperienced father trying to burp a baby.

"I have to admit," a dark-haired man standing near Estebe grinned at Hope, "I'm a little nervous too. Did you know that there were over

13,000 prisoners in this place during the time it was opened, but only ten executions? I think we're fine. Unless there's a killer in our midst."

"Tad, you always know how to make people feel comfortable. Please excuse my brother. He has a sick sense of humor." An older woman took Tad's arm and leaned into the group. "I'm Tamera Johnson. We're from Boise but have never taken the time to tour the prison. Our uncle, Thaddeus, is here from Utah and he suggested we take a family field trip."

Angie stepped forward. "I'm Angie Turner and this is my crew from The County Seat. We're in River Vista."

"I've been to your restaurant. A very nice setting for such a small town. It was a surprise when my husband got us dinner reservations. You have quite a following in the area." Tamera looked around the group. "I don't think I've ever met so many chefs before."

"I just started." Hope explained.

"Hope is our newest addition to the kitchen. She just graduated from the Boise State culinary program." Angie smiled at the girl who, apparently, felt uncomfortable being called a chef. "And this is my boyfriend, Ian. He runs the Farmers' Market co-op in River Vista."

"We're surrounded by food experts. I may just have to bend your ear on this recipe I've been trying to figure out. I can't get it to work like it does at my favorite restaurant." She smiled and nodded to the guard motioning them into the next room. "Looks like we're getting started. See you on the inside."

Ian moved over so the family could follow the guards. Angie noticed a few couples behind them, but they didn't seem in the mood for chatting. In fact, it looked like they were waiting for the lights to go down to get a little closer.

Ian fell in step with Angie. "I think this is going to be an interesting evening."

"I think 'interesting' is an understatement." Angie shivered a little as they went through the open iron gate. When they were all in the large hallway, the guard that brought up the rear pulled the bars closed and clicked the locks shut. The sound echoed in the stone room.

"You are officially residents of the Idaho Penitentiary for the evening. I hope you enjoy your stay." He called over our heads. "Step forward to the light. Harry Orchard was one of our most famous residents. He confessed to killing over seventeen people, including a former Idaho governor. By the end of his life, he was living outside the prison walls in a cottage he'd built himself. He started a shoe shop and a poultry farm inside the prison."

An old sepia photo of an elderly man near a small rock building was posted on their left. A small placard described Harry's crimes, as well as his more redeeming characteristics.

"Over here we have one of Butch Cassidy's boys. Henry 'Bob' Meeks wasn't a long term resident but he tried to make his stay even shorter by escaping. He was shot in the leg, then doctors had to amputate the wounded limb. Later, he tried another method of escape and jumped off the top of a cell house. Finally, he was sent to the asylum." Bridget told the next story.

The tour went on like that with each guard giving the story of a different famous resident. Bridget presented the final story. "There were about 250 women incarcerated here over the years. Lyda Southard was convicted of killing her fourth husband with arsenic. Investigators pulled together evidence to support the premise that the other three husbands, a brother in law, and a son were all killed by the same method."

"She sounds like a peach of a girl," Tad called out. "Just don't eat her apple pie, it's killer."

There were a few laughs but more groans to Tad's joke. He glanced around at the group and muttered, "Tough crowd."

"I think it's sad when women feel they have no other way out besides murder." Hope said.

"Honey, she killed at least five people, including her own child. I think she needed better coping mechanisms," Nancy said.

Hope nodded, then glanced at the photo again. "You're probably right, but it's still sad."

They made their way to the gun collection where the guys were huddled over the display talking. Hope, Angie, Felicia and Nancy grabbed a table in the corner to sit. "I never got the fascination with guns," Nancy admitted. "My ex-husband was a hunter and he had all kinds of weapons. Most that weren't good for hunting at all."

"Well, if the zombie apocalypse happens while we're here, we'll be safe." Hope touched the stone walls. "Can you believe the prisoners built this building? Now they just make license plates."

"I think that's not quite true. I do some prison mission work, and a lot of the woman who are incarcerated are working on their degrees, so they have job skills when they get out. They need something to count on besides the family or man who led them down the wrong path." Nancy fixed her pony tail.

"When do you have time to volunteer?" Angie studied her chef. "Last I heard, you were raising kids and working two jobs."

"I only do it one Sunday a month after church. It helps me remember how lucky I am to have what I have. Even if it is crazy at times." Nancy grinned. "I'm sure the rest of you volunteer too."

Hope nodded. "I'm on the college sorority that works with the homeless in town. Of course, I'm going to have to quit when fall semester starts since I'm not a student anymore. Maybe I should check out your program?"

"Of course, but maybe you could find something where there's more young people involved." Nancy glanced over at the men talking about the gun collection. "We're a bunch of women who aren't trying to build our lives. You need to be around people your age. You already hang with us in the kitchen way too much."

"I like you guys." Hope countered. "Besides, I do a lot of things with friends my age. I'm just going to miss the structure of college. I got my schedule at the beginning of the semester. I took the classes and as long as I passed, I moved on. Now, no one is telling me what I need to do. Not even my folks. Although my little sister made it clear it's time for me to leave home so she can have my room."

Angie laughed. "Out of the mouths of babes. Do you make enough to pay for an apartment? Rents are pretty high right now."

"I have a friend I can move in with. She's been bugging me about sharing an apartment for years. She's a checker over at Winco in Meridian." Hope pointed to the guards who were standing in the corner talking. "Does it look like they're fighting about something? Do you think something went wrong with the tour?"

Angie glance over to the doorway where two of the men were definitely in a heated argument. She couldn't tell what they were saying, but the tone of the voices told her neither party was happy. She glanced at Felicia. "Do you think something's wrong?"

Felicia glanced around the room, then leaned into the table to get everyone's attention. "It's Halloween season. They probably hate staying late just so more people come during the week. Or maybe it's part of the show?"

"If that's true, they're really good actors." Angie heard the low growl come from Dom. He felt the tension in the air just as much as she did. Or he sensed her unease. Either way, it was time to break up the conversation and continue with the tour. "Maybe if we stand up it will look like we're ready to leave the area."

"And maybe pigs will fly. Men only do what they want, when they want." Hope said, then she slapped her hand over her mouth. "I shouldn't have said that."

“That’s fine. We all can say what we don’t mean at times.” Felicia met Angie’s gaze.

Angie thought she could read her friend’s thoughts. Hope never said anything mean or sarcastic. Maybe this prison visit hadn’t been the best idea for a team building event. She stood and Dom moved toward her. “Let’s see if we can get this tour going. Maybe if the guards are busy, they’ll stop sniping at each other.”

“One can only hope,” Nancy called out to the men. “Come on, we’re heading out.”

Matt ran back to Angie like a little puppy. “You can’t believe the displays they have. They must have every gun ever made and several that they used right here when the prison was open.”

“That’s awesome.” She watched as Matt ran to Felicia to report the same information. At least someone was having fun. By the time she got there, the men had moved away from each other and she ran into Officer Bridget. “Is everything okay?”

She sighed, running a hand over her hair. “I take it everyone heard the fight.”

“Not much, but yeah, we knew they weren’t happy. Is there a problem?” Angie took in the woman’s pale face. She looked stressed.

“They’ve been at each other all summer. I guess Marty is dating Pat’s ex-wife. I don’t know what the problem is; he divorced her to go chasing younger women. Now he’s all up in Marty’s face like they’re still married. Marty’s a nice guy. Rachel could do much worse.”

“Relationships are hard, even when they’ve been broken for a while.” Angie was relieved that it wasn’t anything about the tour. “Are we going to be here much longer? I could use a bathroom break.”

“Sure, that’s our next stop. We’ve got refreshments in the main area. We were going to assign you your cells first, but I think I’ll let these two calm down a bit. I’ll round up the troops.”

Angie went back to Felicia while Bridget got everyone’s attention. They were down to two guards, Bridget and the guy that didn’t seem to ever talk. Poor Bridget, it must be like working with caged tigers with the two fighting and the other one not speaking. “I’m so glad we work well together.”

“This group does seem a little dysfunctional.” Felicia nodded. “Did you hear what the fight was about? Rumor has it they are both in love with the same woman.”

“Basically true.” Angie glanced at her friend. “Do you think we need some kind of non-fraternization policy?”

"With me and Estebe? You want him to sign something saying we'll be adults if we break up?" Felicia laughed. "I don't think he'd ever talk to me again, so you wouldn't have to worry about a fight."

"Are you talking about us?" Estebe asked coming up from behind and putting a hand on her shoulder.

Felicia jumped and Angie laughed. "Kind of. I was telling her how much I appreciate our team. You guys are great together."

Estebe's gaze darted to the fake guards at the front of the room. "Not all teams work the same way. Sometimes, it's just a job."

"This is the coolest job in the world." Matt jumped in on the discussion. "Thanks for doing these teambuilding events. I can't wait for next quarter."

"You may regret saying that." Hope's gaze narrowed onto Matt. "It's my turn to schedule and you're going to pay for this one. How do you feel about knitting?"

"You can't make us knit," Matt looked from Hope to Angie then to Estebe. "Seriously, you can't be thinking that would be even an ounce of fun."

"I like learning new crafts." Angie said, then she pointed to the doorway. "Looks like we're moving out. Hope, I look forward to seeing your ideas for the next event."

Estebe slapped Matt on the back. "I think I see some payback in your future."

"This is a great outing. I can't believe she's not having fun."

Estebe narrowed his eyes at Matt.

"Okay so maybe it's not for everyone."

The group moved into the next room. Tables and benches were scattered around the large room. It had a vaulted ceiling and Angie could see three floors of cells circling the area. The tables were screwed to the floor.

Bridget stopped in the middle of the room. "Welcome to the first great room concept. Prisoners ate, talked, and played games here. There were no televisions of course, but the prison library was just over there in that room. You're welcome to check out a book, but make sure you get it back on time. The late fees around here are murder."

This time the group laughed.

Tad looked offended. "Sure, laugh with the girl. I'm thinking it's a matter of reverse discrimination."

"Give it up Tad, you're just not as funny as this pretty little thing is." Thaddeus Paige nodded to Bridget. "Go ahead young lady. Tell us a story. It's my first and probably last time in a prison, I'd like to know what it was like for inmates."

"Okay, so I'll tell you about the day in the life. That way you all will be sure to stay on the straight and narrow. I hear that conditions in the new prison set in the desert out south of Boise still run with an old west philosophy."

"The last time I was there, it was more like Club Med," a man called from the back. Everyone turned to see who'd spoken and with the attention totally on him, he blushed. "Sorry, I was joking. I've never even had a parking ticket."

Angie hoped the rest of the attendees were as clean as this guy. Otherwise, their night in lockup might just turn into a mess. Besides, what kind of criminal would want to be locked up for a night?

Angie tried to focus on Bridget's story, but she just couldn't shake the unease that had overcome her when they entered the facility.

Chapter 3

An hour later, they were alone in their row of cells. They had four cells near the guard station, with a walkway overlooking the community room. Each cell had two twin beds so Angie shared with Ian, Felicia shared with Estebe, Hope and Nancy had a cell, and Matt had his own cell.

"I can sleep half the night in one cot, then move to the second one if it's not comfortable." Matt put sheets on both beds in his cell. "Unless someone wants to come share with me?"

"We're fine where we are." Hope said and Nancy chuckled.

Estebe stood near the bars. "Are you afraid because you're alone in there? I could have brought one of my nephew's teddy bears."

"Or maybe Dom can sleep with you?" Ian offered.

Matt smoothed the blanket on the first bed. "How did my joy at being on my own get misinterpreted as me being lonely? I do sleep alone in my apartment every night."

"Please, I don't need to hear about your love life." Felicia giggled.

A scream sounded down the hall toward the great room. They all quickly gathered in the hallway. Estebe pointed to the exit near the walkway. "It came from that way?"

"Are you sure? The sounds seem to echo here." Felicia glanced down the hallway the other way. She shook her head. "I don't hear anything that way."

"Who has a flashlight? Maybe this is our first game of the night? We could be part of a scavenger hunt they didn't advertise." Matt returned to his cell and came out with two large flashlights. "Who needs one?"

Estebe took one, glaring at Matt as he did. "I didn't bring one. I guess I should have thought this out more closely."

"I have one on my phone." Felicia reached for her back pocket but her hand came back empty. "And my phone is locked up."

"I didn't know they'd take them." Hope's voice seemed a little too high pitched.

As Angie stepped closer, she saw Nancy put an arm around the young chef. "Don't worry about it. Two flashlights are enough."

"Three." Ian pulled out one from his backpack. "I'm glad I didn't stuff this in the locker."

"Didn't you guys read the inmate list? It said we could bring up to two flashlights and that we might need them if the power went out during our stay." Matt shook his head. "I knew we should have had a pre-meeting to make sure everyone was prepared."

"Are we going to stand here talking, or go find out who screamed?" Ian nodded to Estebe. "You go first, then Matt, you take the middle and I'll come around the back."

"I'm not staying here alone." Hope held on to Estebe's arm.

"No one's asking you to. If you want to come, just get between me and Matt," Estebe said, his voice patient. "Ian was placing the flashlights."

Of course, that wasn't what Ian was doing, Angie could see it in his eyes. But then again, leaving three women behind in the dark wasn't a great plan either. "Let's all go. That way, we're prepared for anything. Dom, come."

She clicked the leash on him and stayed back with Ian as the rest of the group made their way down the hall. She waited until Estebe and Hope were out of earshot and leaned close. "You don't think this is a prank."

"Something's been nagging at me all night. There's something off about our guards *and* our guests. Did you see how Thaddeus wouldn't even look at Tad? That's strange. And the two couples, they're just looking for a place to do it so they can tell their friends. They have no interest in the tour. Or the history of the place." Ian kept shining the light behind them as they kept pace with the group. "And the guards, they're like an episode of Dive Bar Escapades."

"I like dive bars." Angie put her arm in his and watched Dom sniff his way down the hallway. "Besides, dating a co-worker's ex will get you in a fight no matter where you work."

"You have to admit, your team members are the most normal people here." He glanced down at her. "Besides the two of us, that is."

"Sure, start with the sweet talk. Just because we're sharing a cell doesn't mean you get to move over to my side of the room. Dom will be watching." She squeezed his hand.

"It had crossed my mind."

Another scream came from in front of them and they quickened their pace. The group was crowded around the doorway to the library. When Angie got closer, she saw a pair of uniform legs sticking out and blood pooling on the floor. She leaned in to check the guard's face and realized it was Pat. The ex-husband. Had Marty tired of Pat's interference in his new girlfriend's life? "Is he…"

Estebe shook his head. "He's dead."

"He has a cell phone on his belt. Use it to call nine-one-one." Angie pointed to the place where the cell had been earlier in the night. "Wait, it's gone. Maybe it fell off when he was killed. Look around, everyone."

"There's nothing around him except for blood." Hope said taking a few steps back. "I think I might be sick."

"Angie, Felicia – you guys take Hope and go find Bridget and the other guards. Ian, you go too. Matt, Nancy and I will stay here with him." Estebe moved away from the body and pointed to a table. "We'll sit there because we can see all of the exits from that spot. Make sure they call for help before they come back. We need everyone to gather together. There's safety in numbers."

"You don't think someone's just going to kill us off, one by one, do you?" Hope's eyes widened. "I don't even like horror movies."

"Let's just assume he fell. We don't know if he was murdered or not, but we aren't professionals." Ian glanced at Angie. "Let's go so we can get everyone rounded up. Maybe we can hit Denny's on the way home and get some coffee. I'd love a cup of strong coffee right now."

Angie knew Ian was just chattering. Pat's death had everyone on their last nerve. She put a hand on his arm. "Coffee would be awesome, but first, let's go find the guards."

They finally found Marty and Bridget in the gun room. They were sitting at the same table Angie and the others sat at earlier. Bridget looked up in surprise when the group came in. "What are you guys doing out of your cells? I thought you'd all be asleep by now."

"There is a problem." Ian started, swallowed, then looked at Angie.

She nodded, letting him know she'd continue the story. "Your friend, the other guard, Pat?"

"Oh, God. What has he done now? I thought I'd saw him eyeing your young friend. He's basically harmless, he just likes to flirt." Bridget stepped toward him.

"He's a pig. He was always cheating on Rachel with whoever would have him. He needs to have his access to women restricted to like, none." Marty stood and followed her. "Where is he?"

"In the library. Well, almost in the library. Look, it wasn't a problem with him hitting on Hope. He appears to be dead." Angie thought about softening the wording, but she couldn't think of any other word that meant the same thing. Dead was dead. Maybe she was as stressed as Ian.

"He's probably just playing a prank on someone." Bridget smiled but then it dropped off her face. "Wait, you're not kidding. You really think he's dead."

"We checked for a pulse. Where's a phone? We need to call the authorities." Ian sounded better, stronger. They weren't alone in the knowledge any more.

"Pat has the phone. We only keep one phone on hand for the tour because it messes with the authenticity of the event. He's got the key to the gate too." Marty walked toward the door to the hallway. "We'll just move you guys out to the courtyard and then the police can handle the investigation."

"There was no phone." Angie reached out for Marty's arm as he started past her. "What if the killer also took the keys?"

"Then he has to be one of us. Only the guards knew about the phone and the keys. We keep them together with one person so that no one gets caught trying to Google something or sneak out to their car for a cigarette." Marty paused. "The phone has GPS, we can track it."

"Okay, let's go to the library, then we can break off and some of us can go to wherever your GPS tracker is so we can find the phone." Angie sighed. This was getting super complicated. They weren't stranded in a desert, but they might as well have been.

"Sounds like a plan." Bridget nodded at Angie. "Let's make sure there's nothing we can do for Pat. Close the door to the library so no one goes in, and find the GPS and then the phone."

Angie hoped it would be that easy, but past experience told her it was going to be a long night. "Should we wake up the others and bring them down to the common room?"

"I'm sure we're not dealing with some sort of crazy killer. Besides, we don't even know if Pat is dead or maybe he just hit his head really hard. Everything could be back to normal by the time we get to the library." Bridget held her arm out to move them along. "Let's go."

Angie stepped into the hallway first and almost tripped over a portrait easel. "Who moved this here? That wasn't here when we came into the room. Unless we left by another door?"

Ian shined a light at the picture of Lyda Southard. "This was in the gallows room, right?"

Bridget nodded and then realized no one but Angie, just two feet away, could see her in the darkened hallway. "Yes, the painting should be there. Someone's definitely playing tricks on us."

"A trick that got someone dead."

Marty moved the painting over near the wall. "I'll handle this later. Don't get worked up, we have a man to save. I just hope I can get the warden to see what's going on. He's kind of black and white in his thinking."

"What do you think is going on?" Bridget asked Marty as he took off. They left Angie and Ian in the hallway next to Lyda's portrait. If Marty answered her, Angie hadn't heard it.

She turned to Ian. "This is seriously weird. Can we even start to hope this is all a big practical joke on us? That this man is still alive somewhere?"

"You always try to see the bright side, but no, I looked at Pat. That guy is dead. And someone in this locked facility killed him. We're staying together and not letting anyone or anything break us up." Ian took her by the arm and led her away from the moving art work.

"Sounds like a good plan." Angie heard a noise behind them and whirled to look. Nothing stared back at her, but she still had the feeling of being watched. Maybe they had been after Pat and, now that he was gone, the killer would be done as well. She knew she was a Pollyanna, but it had served her well for most of her life.

"Marty appears to be the only one with a motive to kill Pat, right?" She asked Ian who was walking ahead of her.

"Right, but we don't know he was killed." Ian muttered. "He might have slipped and fallen."

"And the phone just disappeared?" Angie shook her head. "Improbable."

Ian slowed down and looked at her. "Marty seemed to be the only person with a grudge. Who would kill someone after having a very public fight?"

"Exactly." Angie didn't say anything else. She was working it out in her mind. It didn't make sense to take the phone and the key unless they didn't want anyone to get out. Which meant one thing to her. The killings weren't done.

When they got back to the common room, Estebe stood up and looked at Felicia who moved closer to Hope. It was obvious to Angie that their newest chef was having problems dealing with this death. She'd been around death before, but she'd never seen the body after life seeped out of it and on to the floor.

The two guards finished examining the body, moved it inside the library and shut the door behind them. They stayed inside the room for a while.

"What do you think they're doing?" Felicia leaned over the table toward Angie.

Angie shrugged. "I don't know, but I have a bad feeling about this. If one or both of them are the killer, they could be destroying evidence."

"With a room full of witnesses?" Estebe scoffed. "I don't think they are that dumb."

"Maybe, but I am concerned about the missing key and phone. If the killer is the only one with a phone or the key to escape, what's preventing him from just leaving us in here forever?" She met everyone's gaze but no one answered her at first.

The fourth guard came out from the hallway. "I can answer that. The doors are all unlocked at six am, no matter what. It was a safety feature that the historical society insisted on setting up before the first lock in. They didn't want something bad to happen and it be on their watch."

"Where have you been?" Angie asked the man. "And what's your name? You never introduced yourself."

"Sorry, I'm Glen. I was getting the honeymooners settled. Did you know that both of the other couples just got married today? They're friends and I guess they came straight from the courthouse. I don't think we'll see any of them until the alarm sounds for the end of the lockdown." Glen chuckled as he glanced around the table. "Why are you guys down from your cells? Did you need coffee or something? We have several sets of cards in the library if you want to play, but the light isn't really good here in the community room."

"There's been a murder." Hope said, her tone subdued, but at least she sounded calm. "Do you have the phone to call for help?"

"A murder?" Glen chuckled. "Is this a game? Which one of our prisoners got it? Or were they the killers?"

The door to the library opened, and Marty and Bridget walked out. They walked over to the table and Bridget sank onto a bench. "The key's not with him."

"Wait. Pat has the phone and the key. Are you telling me that something happened to hard as nails Pat?" Glen looked from Bridget to Marty. His gaze went to Hope. "That he was murdered?"

"He's dead. I don't know how, but yeah. And the phone and key are gone." Marty studied Glen. "Unless you have them."

"No man, I wasn't scheduled to be responsible for another hour." He ran a hand through his hair. "I can't believe the last thing I said to him was 'Stop being a jerk'."

Chapter 4

"Should we wake up the others?" Felicia glanced around the table. The remaining guards looked shell shocked.

"Why? So they can be as scared as we are?" Glen stood and took his cup over to the coffee pot that Bridget brought out of the employee break room. He emptied the pot, then started to make a fresh pot. "I can't believe this really happened. Especially on this night. We shouldn't have let them schedule a tour tonight."

"What's so special about tonight?" Matt played with a deck of cards he'd found in the break room. No one had wanted to go back in the library.

"Glen, that's just urban legend," Bridget warned.

Glen came back to his place at the table and pointed his cup in the direction of the library. "Tell that to Pat over there."

"It's stupid." Bridget insisted.

"Tell us the story." Matt pressed. "We've got eight hours until the doors unlock. We might as well be entertained."

"You might regret that statement, but I think it's an avenue of interest." Glen sipped his coffee. "So we told you about Lyda. What we didn't tell you was the other story. Lyda got pregnant and delivered a baby girl in prison."

"You mean she was pregnant when she came into the facility?" Felicia asked.

Glen shook his head. "Nope. She had relations with a guard. Consensual, at least that was the rumor. When she delivered the baby, someone told her she'd be able to keep it. To raise it inside these walls. But they lied. When the baby was three days old, they came for her. And Lyda threw a fit. She threatened to kill everyone if her baby wasn't returned to her. Especially the guard who gotten her in that condition in the first place."

"And the baby wasn't returned." Hope guessed.

"Right on the money. By that time, the baby was already with a new family. When the full moon came out that next week, the guard who'd fathered the child was found murdered. Stabbed."

Bridget shook her head. "They couldn't prove it was Lyda. She was in her cell all night long according to the cell records. But there weren't cameras back then, so the jailer could have been bought off."

"Okay, so that's strange, but there must have been a lot of unexplained deaths in the time this place was open." Ian stood. "And I agree with Felicia, we should have everyone together."

"You haven't heard the rest of the story. Every year on the night before Halloween, a light is seen going through the prison. I've seen it when I was locking up. They had to pay us triple time to work this shift. Everyone knows that Lyda's ghost walks these halls this night. And I guess Pat got in her way. Or reminded her of the baby's father." Glen sipped his coffee. "And that's the story of our most famous ghost."

A bang sounded next to Matt and everyone around the table jumped. He leaned down and picked up a book. Grinning at everyone, he said, "Boo."

"That wasn't nice, Matt." Hope slapped his arm. "You scared me."

"Just sound effects for Glen's ghost story." Matt grinned.

Just then a scream echoed from the cell bank.

"Another sound effect?" Estebe asked.

"No, that was a real scream." Marty jumped up, sloshing coffee on the table. "I just can't tell where it came from."

"We'll divide into groups. I want all of you with one of us. I think the idea of waking the others has become mandatory." Bridget stood and started pointing at people. "You two go with Marty – take the top floor of the cells. Glen, you take these two and take the middle row. The rest of you come with me. We'll search the entire downstairs, starting with the cells."

Matt pointed to the library. "Don't you think you should keep someone with the body, I mean, Pat?"

Bridget turned to look at the closed door. "I don't think he's getting up to leave anytime soon, but you're right. In case we're all wrong and he's not dead, someone should stay here."

Matt, Angie and Estebe looked at each other. They were the group assigned to go with Bridget and since there were three of them, it made sense that the person staying behind should be from their group.

"I'll stay. I brought it up. I'll be on zombie watch." Matt sank back onto the bench with a quick glance at the door. "But if I wind up dead, I think you should rename the restaurant in my honor and put up a plaque telling everyone what a hero I was."

Angie patted him on the back. "Done. But you know the only reason I'd agree with something like that is the chance of you dying is slim to none. I love the County Seat, just as it is."

Matt shuffled the cards. "Just go already. Now Glen's story has me revisiting all my past relationships for bad deeds that someone might want to make me pay for."

"You did dump that girl at the fair a couple of years ago. That was cruel." Hope smiled at him while her group was leaving. When he glared back at her she giggled, and called back, "Just trying to help."

Bridget motioned to Angie and Estebe to follow her and they went toward the main cell doors. "Watch your step. Some of the stone floors have settled and are uneven."

"Understood." Since Angie didn't have a flashlight like Bridget and Estebe, she fell into the middle of the two. "How long have you worked here?"

"Since I got out of college. I was a drama major and had big Hollywood dreams. But then I interned here and fell in love with the history of Idaho. I do several historical reenactments every year for the society so with my salary and the extra I get for the other events, I make a good wage. Not Hollywood money, but enough to live comfortably here." She had a wistfulness to her voice.

"Was that the only reason you didn't try to hit the big screen?" Angie knew she was being personal but it kept her mind off of rampaging ghosts with a mission of revenge.

"My mom was sick the last two years of college. So I stayed around." Bridget paused at the first cell and shined her light into the emptiness. "When she passed, I had a house, a job, and a life here. I wasn't the new kid on the block so I just stayed. Man, I haven't thought about how pathetic my life must look for a long time."

"Your life is fine, if you're doing what you want to do. I had a restaurant in San Francisco for a while and I learned that people are the same everywhere you go. So I came home. We have a crew of chefs who love food and cooking just as much as I do." Angie wondered if it was the dark hallways that were driving her to talk about dreams and goals and life plans. Maybe it was the choices that the inmates made that imprisoned them here, and the fact that they were unable to live a life outside the stone walls that moved her.

"I could walk away from cooking anytime and live comfortably for the rest of my life." Estebe admitted from his place behind the women. "But I like having a purpose. I like contributing to the team where I work. I like keeping Matt in line."

Angie laughed at that. When Bridget shined her light into a cell, she saw something in the corner. "Wait, shine that over here."

Angie moved into the cell and underneath the bed was an old-fashioned baby rattle. The silver was tarnished, but the ball inside still made noise when she picked it up. She held it out to Bridget. "Is this one of your antiques?"

Bridget stepped closer to Angie but didn't take the rattle. "Not that I've ever seen. I mean, it might have been in the storeroom, but it shouldn't be out here."

"Maybe Glen put it out to beef up his ghost story. He was gone from the group for a long time." Estebe noted. "He could have planted it."

"But how would he have known that we'd go searching for someone screaming?" Bridget shook her head. "Glen's a good guy. Too quiet and he doesn't take the drama part of the job seriously, but he wouldn't play with us. Especially not after what happened to Pat."

"But he didn't know Pat was dead when he was gone." Angie studied the rattle. It had initials carved into the silver. BDP. She read them aloud. "Anyone you know?"

"Not a clue. So can we continue? Or do you want to look for more baby items?" Bridget stepped out of the cell and crossed the hallway to the next one. "This one is clear."

Estebe nodded to Angie to move ahead of him. When she went to lay the rattle down on the bed, he spoke. "Keep it. It might be important."

She tucked it in her jacket pocket and stepped out into the hallway. Bridget was waiting for them.

"Ten cells done on this side. Twenty more to go." She sighed as she checked the next cell. "I was hoping for a quiet night. I even brought a book I've been dying to read. I'm behind on my Stephen King. Man, he's releasing fast lately."

"I guess you're just going to have to deal with a real mystery tonight." Angie thought about all the investigations she'd done since she'd moved back home. She'd thought she'd be working, cooking, and gardening when she returned. Instead she had been-in Sheriff Brown's words-sticking her nose into things that didn't concern her. She assumed the well-meaning sheriff wouldn't fault her for this adventure. She hadn't signed up the crew to be part of a murder investigation. Things just happened that way. At least to her.

The Johnson siblings and their uncle occupied the next set of cells. Or at least they should have been there. Tamera slept on top of one of the cots, snoring. In the next cell, Thaddeus, the uncle, sat smoking a cigarette.

"Is it morning already? Thank God. I can't believe how much noise that girl is making. I haven't slept a wink all night." He stood and took another pull on his cigarette.

"Smoking is not allowed in the cells," Bridget snapped. "How did you get those inside? Didn't anyone tell you to leave them in your locker?"

"Little girl, I've been smoking two packs a day for most of my life. Do you think I go anywhere without a pack on me? I'd start going through withdrawal in less than an hour." He grabbed his backpack and put out the cigarette on the stone floor. At least he picked up the butt and put it in his pocket. "Wake up Sleeping Beauty there and my idiot nephew and let's get out of here. This is the last time I let them plan the activities on my visit."

"Sir, it's not time to leave, but we do need all of you to gather with us in the common room. Gather your stuff and we'll wake the others." Bridget pointed to Angie. "You wake up the female."

"Her name is Tamera." Angie said flatly. Bridget was too involved in her role as guard. Angie was surprised she hadn't said female inmate. She moved into Tamera's cell and shook the woman gently.

"What's going on?" She said, her words garbled.

"We need you to come with us. There's been an incident." Angie said gently, "Slip on your shoes and grab your stuff."

"Where's Tad?" Tamera moved like she hadn't been asleep. "Is my brother all right?"

Angie sat the backpack that had been on the floor on the bed while Tamera slipped on her shoes. "I'm sure he's in his cell sleeping. Is there something going on?"

"Yes, there is." Estebe leaned on the cell doorway. "Tad's not in his cell and it looks like the bed hasn't been slept in."

"Oh, my God. What happened to him?" Tamera moved toward the door, but Estebe blocked it.

"Answer one question first, why was the first thing you asked about when you woke up about your brother? Is he in trouble?" Estebe kept his voice calm, but it held a measure of authority.

The older man laughed. "That boy was born in trouble. He's been in more jail cells than this one in his life, I tell you that. My brother went bankrupt trying to keep him out of prison."

"Tad didn't do those things he was charged with. His friends were the problem, not him, but he got blamed. They all ganged up on him." Tamera shot back at her uncle. Anger seemed in every word.

"You're believing his line of bull crap. He's always been a liar and a thief. What did he do this time? Is something missing?"

"Thanks for the vote of confidence, Uncle Thaddeus." Tad came walking toward them from the back of the cell block. "I've been reading at the end of the hall. I didn't want my light to disturb you."

Angie and Estebe exchanged glances. They just cleared that area and hadn't seen Tad. Reading or otherwise.

"Grab your stuff and let's all go into the common room." Bridget said, ignoring the family drama. But Angie knew Tad wasn't reading where he said he'd been. She just let that statement ride. She wanted to get him in the common room without incident.

Their group hadn't found the screamer, but they rounded up three of the guests. And one had a shady alibi.

They dropped the three off with Matt in the common room. He looked relieved to see them, then hesitated when Bridget said they had one more area to clear. "Maybe someone else should stay with me?"

Bridget glanced at Tad and nodded. "You're right. We don't need three of us checking out the rest of the area. Estebe, why don't you stay with Matt? Angie and I will be right back."

Estebe traded glances with Angie but when she nodded, he sat down on the bench. "Have you ever played Texas Holdem? We don't have chips, but I could get you ready to come join one of our Wednesday night poker games."

"Probably so the guy can fleece you of your paycheck." Thaddeus moved over to the table with Estebe and Matt. "I'll sit in too, just to make sure he teaches you right."

As they moved away from the table and back into the areas where the tour had started, Angie spoke quietly. "Tad wasn't back there reading."

"I know."

"Why would he lie?" Angie shined the flashlight she now carried into the gun display room. It looked empty, but she followed Bridget inside.

"That is a very good question." She sat at one of the tables. Angie stared at her. "Come sit by me. I want to go over what we've found out so far."

"I thought we were looking for someone who might be hurt?" Angie glanced around the room. It was clearly empty besides the two of them.

"The scream didn't come from this way. It came from the cell block. Either Glen or Marty will find the woman. Right now, I'm confused about what's going on. What do you know about the three of them?"

"The new arrivals? Is that what you're talking about?" Angie clarified.

When Bridget nodded, Angie leaned back in her chair, thinking about what she knew. "I talked to Tamera at the beginning of the tour. She said her uncle was visiting from Utah and they thought it would be fun to go on the tour." Angie paused. Was that right? Is that what Tamera said? Who brought up the tour? It didn't seem like Tad would have suggested it, especially with his record. Visiting a prison wouldn't be first on an ex-con's list. "Anyway, that was about it. They're here as a family bonding exercise."

"Not much bonding going on. I wonder if the old man has money. The others don't seem too attached to him, and it might just be about keeping on his good side for the will." Bridget was making notes in her little notebook. "Do you know the other two couples?"

"Not at all. They didn't seem like they wanted to be part of any conversation, besides with each other. I heard they just got married, but you heard that too, from Glen." Angie thought about Glen's arrival in the great room after the murder. He said he'd been held up getting the couples situated but that wouldn't have taken much time. Especially if all they wanted to do was be alone. She shivered. The thought of making love in a prison on your wedding night seemed a little dark. Okay, *a lot* dark. But maybe people liked a less perfect honeymoon atmosphere. She watched Bridget as she considered her notes. "How long has Glen worked here?"

"Oh, we've all been around the same amount of time, five to seven years. I know, it sounds more like a sentence rather than a career, but we all enjoy it. And most nights, we get a lot of time on our own. I'm writing a book. Marty's working on a screenplay. And Pat, well, he liked watching sports on his tablet." Bridget continued writing as she talked.

"You didn't mention Glen." Angie didn't think any of the guards could have done this, but she needed to cross off all the suspects. Right now, Glen was on top of her list for his lateness to the employee break room conversations.

"Glen is a history buff. He would take his notes from the last book he'd read about the prison or the inmates and search the grounds to find what cells people had been assigned to. He eventually started a timeline for all the residents he'd studied just in case family members wanted to know what he'd learned. I told him he needed to publish it, but I think he saw it as a way to give back to the prison. I guess you'd call it community service."

"What, was he in jail too?"

"Oh, no. But he liked to give back to the community." Bridget's laugh made Angie feel like she was barking up the wrong tree.

Bridget closed her notebook and stuffed it in her back pocket. "I guess we better finish our walk through and get back to the common room. Maybe we can find out more about these honeymooners without anyone getting suspicious."

Angie thought the chance of anyone getting between two honeymooners was probably non-existent, but she'd let Bridget deal with that conversation.

Chapter 5

The honeymooners were Nick and Sara and Jamie and Liz. And they were all in the same paranormal hunting group. Nick had brought an EMF sensor and between snuggling with his new wife, he'd been tracking the ghost levels for the evening.

"I haven't had much of a blip except for twice. One about an hour ago and one just a few minutes ago." Nick pointed to his notebook where he'd noted levels every fifteen minutes except when a surge occurred. Then the timing when down to every five minutes. "I thought it might be an issue with the electricity in the building or nearby."

"Did you hear a woman scream about ten minutes ago?" Angie stood next to him, glancing at his notebook. "It would have been just about the same time as your last surge."

"No." Nick's eyes widened and he turned to the rest of his group. "What about you guys? Did you hear anything?"

"Not a peep. Well, except for Liz's giggling." Jamie grinned at his wife. "I found out she's pretty ticklish."

Ian caught Angie's gaze and shrugged.

"There isn't anyone else in here, is there?" Angie turned back to Bridget. "A woman or someone who screams like a girl?"

"Not that I know. This is everyone who should be here. Well, except the old man." Glen glanced around the room. "Where did he take off to?"

"The bathroom. That guy lives in the bathroom. He'll be there all night." Tad grumbled. "That's why I don't invite him to stay with me anymore. Dude, I need access to the toilet once in a while."

"Tad, that's disrespectful. Uncle Thaddeus is older. Things don't move as well as they do when you're younger." Tamera chided her brother. "I'm sure he'll be back as soon as he can."

"If he's gone more than ten minutes, I'll go check on him. I think we need to stay close together." Marty glanced around at the shadows at the edge of the common room. "No need for anyone else to get hurt by accident."

"There's no way you can think that," Matt pointed to the library, "was an accident."

"We aren't trained investigators. When the doors open in the morning and the police investigators look at the scene, then we'll know for sure," Bridget said. She nodded to Glen and Marty. "Let's go see if we can find a phone in the break room. Maybe someone left their cell."

Ian watched as they walked away. "That's highly unlikely. I'm getting the impression that our guards have a few secrets they don't want us to know. Or they're talking about us."

"Could be either one." Estebe said. "Although Marty has the best motive since he was dating Pat's wife. I'm feeling that Glen might just be our killer. He's not truthful in his revelations of his whereabouts."

"I'm feeling the same way." Ian glanced around the room. "Let's go sit over at that table. Maybe we can get the rest of the group to follow? I'd like to know their take on this."

"Without us looking like we're separating ourselves from the others? No. But I guess we can try. It's not like we know these people at all." Angie caught Hope's gaze and then nodded toward Matt and Nancy. Then she pointed to the table on the far side of the room. Loudly, so everyone could hear, she said, "Since we're stuck here and not sleeping, let's go over the menu planning for tomorrow night's service. I think, when we get out of here, I'm going to sleep for a while before I come in to work and we might not have time to get this together then."

Felicia stood from where she'd been sitting. "Angie, sometimes you're such a freaking slave driver. You know everyone's tired."

"Yeah, but no one's sleeping, so let's get this done." Angie turned to Tamera. "Sorry, we'll take the discussion over there so it won't bother you all. Menu discussions can get a little heated, especially since my sous chef thinks he knows everything."

"I heard that," Estebe called from the table. "And you're right, I do know everything. Glad you finally acknowledged my superior knowledge about local foods."

Angie rolled her eyes for the others' benefit, then mumbled as she walked toward the group. "Estebe can be a real jerk."

When she sat down, the crew at the table was staring down at the floor. One by one they looked up, gave her a quick grin, then dropped their eyes. Matt glanced over at the rest of the people in the room. "No one's watching."

"That you can tell," Estebe corrected. "Let's talk about soups for a minute, then we should be fine."

The group discussed the three soups they wanted to prepare this month. There was strong support for both last year's russet and sweet potato soup and the lamb stew Estebe had brought to the menu. "I'd really like something new this fall. I know we're already through October, but maybe one more? Everyone brings an idea for next week's family meal and we'll take the decision to the table."

"With that settled, we wanted to ask the rest of you about your feelings regarding the killer. Any ideas?" Ian leaned into the group and Angie glanced across the room. No one was watching them.

"The first person you suspect. Just a name, not why." She pointed at Matt.

"Marty."

Then one by one she pointed to the rest of them. When they had gone around the table, Marty had four votes, Glen had two votes, and Tad had one. She looked at the names Felicia had written down. "Marty people, why?"

Matt shrugged. "Pat was giving him a hard time with the girl. If she'd changed her mind and gone back to him, Marty would be out in the cold. It's hard to fight against exes and history."

"Anyone else?"

Nancy shook her head. "It doesn't feel like Marty. He seems to be a nice guy."

"Okay, anyone else who did vote for Marty have a different reason?" She watched while Ian, Felicia, and Estebe shook their heads. "So the jealousy and keeping what's now mine motive."

"Nancy, you and I said Glen. Why did you pick him?" Angie knew her reason for choosing Glen, but she didn't know Nancy's.

"Glen was missing too long. He avoided answering direct questions. And," Nancy flushed but continued, "this is stupid, but he reminds me of my ex. He's definitely hiding something."

Angie nodded. She'd felt it too. There was a secret hanging around Glen's neck, and he wouldn't let it go easily.

Ian turned to Hope. "So why did you choose Tad?"

"Besides being an ex-con? He doesn't like his uncle. Or his sister for that matter. He's always making faces at her behind her back. Then he sucks up when she's looking. Anyone that mean, he has to be the killer. The other people are nice. Tad doesn't have a nice bone in his body, as my grandmother would say." Hope leaned back in her chair and folded her arms. No one was going to mess with her logic.

"I don't think we made any ground in ruling anyone out." Angie looked at the others. "Maybe we should ask some questions and see if we can eliminate at least a few of the players."

"Sounds like a plan. Let's all take one person and go talk to them. Then we'll come back here and compare notes. Someone has got to have an alibi." Ian glanced at Angie. "What do you say, want to call a break?"

"Just as soon as we divide up the names." She wrote down the names of everyone in the room, then handed the notebook to Felicia. "Write your name next to someone you think you can get to chat. Then pass it to the next person. We can try to get to everyone in the room before the guards come back. We may have to do a second round. Or a few of us will."

She watched as everyone scribbled their names by the suspects'. She glanced at the name left when it came around. She had Uncle Thaddeus. "Thanks guys."

"If you wanted an easy assignment, you should have picked first, before you passed around the notebook." Ian shook his head. "What were you thinking?"

"I guess I wasn't." Angie admitted. She stood and called out. "Ten-minute break. Don't take off."

"Where would we go? We're locked in, remember?" Felicia said in her best bored valley girl tone.

Angie tried not to smile. Her team could pull the wool over anyone's eyes-which may or may not be a good thing. She went to the coffee pot, glanced around the room, and decided not to sit by anyone from her group. She sighed loudly as she sat next to Thaddeus who was playing with the deck of cards that Matt had found.

"Your team seems to be dissolving. You ever think of firing the whole lot of them and starting over? It's worked for me several times in my career." Thaddeus didn't look up from his game of Solitaire.

Angie snorted. "I would, but one of the trouble makers is dating my partner. And she's not going to let me get rid of the guy. So what business were you in?"

"Sales. I sold just about everything through my years, except for electronics and those damn computers. They said I wasn't smart enough to sell computers. Hell, I could sell ice to Eskimos."

"You should have seen the guy who sold us our accounting system. He had to be twelve. And he didn't know anything. I swear, wisdom isn't considered when they're giving out jobs today." Angie sipped her coffee and stared at Estebe who was talking to Tad. "Especially if you have a pretty face."

"Exactly. You can be a total air head and they'll hire you if you're under thirty." Thaddeus sighed. "It's not even like I need the money, but I sure miss going to work every day. I've been looking for a new place ever since I was laid off three years ago. I think they see my age when I walk into an interview and my résumé gets thrown in the circular file."

"Too bad you're not a chef. I could use a strong hand in my kitchen." She shot a look at Estebe. "One that I could trust."

"I'd burn water." He smiled holding a card up in the air and considering his choices. He threw it on the discard pile. "My late wife used to tell me that all the time. I'd burn water. She's been gone for a few years now. I'm glad she's not here to see what happened to me. Now, all I have time to do is genealogy. It's kind of interesting finding out who you are by going back in time."

"So who are you related to? Anyone famous?" Angie leaned forward, focusing on her fake excitement. She couldn't over do this.

"Nah. Not really famous. Kind of a local big shot, but no one as big as Simplot or anything."

Simplot was the local potato king who'd made his money selling frozen fries to McDonald's. Now, the massive company he'd built had a whole line of produce-based products. They took the basic potato and processed it so it lost its flavor and natural goodness. But maybe that was just her farm to table mentality kicking in. She brushed imaginary lint off her jeans, looking bored. "Oh, that's nice."

He frowned, probably realizing he'd lost her attention. "But I can tell you that you'd be amazed if you heard. It's kind of funny me being in here where it all started."

"What's that supposed to mean?" Angie didn't want to sound too greedy, but she had the feeling that Thaddeus was telling her something important.

"You'll find out sooner or later." He winked at her and then stood. "I need to find the little boys' room."

She watched him walk away and replayed the conversation in her head. Apparently, Thaddeus found out that he was descended from someone important. Maybe someone who had been an inmate here?

Felicia waved at her from the other table. "I thought you said ten minutes?"

Angie joined the others at the table. "Anyone get anything interesting?"

"Nick used to be an MMA fighter. He gave it up when he met Sara." Ian said in a low voice.

"Sara said they got a call from the historical society and they were gifted free tours because both were part of the paranormal investigator group. Whoever gifted them the tour thought it would be cool to have them here on Lyda's night. That's what they call tonight since most of the sightings happen this date." Hope shook her head. "You should talk to them. They are convinced this is all about the death of the real guard so many years ago."

"That's stupid. Why would a ghost kill a fake guard? So yeah, he was a jerk, but so are a lot of other people. I talked to Sara after you did, Hope. She, on the other hand, isn't a true believer but her husband Nick is. She's hoping to wean him from this hobby now that they're married." Nancy shook her head. "Never marry someone you're going to try to change. Love them like they are or just move on."

"Personal experience with that?" Felicia asked but with a smile.

"Definitely. Although it was my husband trying to change me." Nancy sipped her coffee. "Didn't work."

"Don't tell me you're a paranormal groupie in your free time?" Estebe asked.

Nancy barked out a laugh. "What free time? No, he wanted me to be a stay at home mom and make an amazing life off one income. No matter how small his check was. He didn't get that braces cost money. Not to mention college."

Hope nodded her head. "My folks have been drilling 'College isn't a free ride' into our heads for so long. I've had a summer job since I could babysit. And, because of the money they set aside and my earnings, I left school without any student loan debt. I want to buy a better car, but I'm saving for it because I don't want a loan."

"That's great Hope. Now, did Sara say anything else?" Angie gently steered the conversation back to the suspects.

"Not anything that seemed strange." Hope smiled, "She does love her husband though. She watched him like a hawk all the time we were talking and he was talking to Ian."

Angie filed that under honeymoon weirdness. She turned to her friend. "Felicia? Anything more out of Tamera?"

"She apologized for her brother not once or twice even. She apologized ten times, which was hard to do in less than ten minutes. She says he's a little freaked out about his life this year. But he's on a good path."

Everyone looked at each other.

"Just because the sister is worried doesn't mean he's our killer." Angie reminded them even though she wanted to scream it was the final straw.

She wasn't sure she had enough facts to even have a police officer question him. She checked her list. "Matt? What about Jamie? Any skeletons there?"

"Not a one. He's a good guy under all those preppy clothes. He loves his ghost stories though. He and Liz are taking off in an RV in a week to go visit a bunch of haunted places. Liz is writing a book." Matt paused, looking up at the ceiling. "And that's all he told me. Well, except the fact Nick and Sara were supposed to ride along, but she put the kibosh on the plans this morning."

"Never going to last." Nancy said.

"Okay, thanks for the report, Matt." She looked down at her list. She needed to report her news and Estebe hadn't talked yet. "Estebe? What about Tad?"

"That man is a self-consumed jerk who should never be around people again. He said he hoped this place was haunted, and he hoped his uncle would have a heart attack when he saw the real ghost." Estebe sighed. "I do not like the man. I wish he had killed the guard another day. One where we weren't here."

Chapter 6

"Do you really think Tad killed Pat?" Angie stared at Estebe. He wasn't looking at anyone at the table. Instead he was watching the others.

"I think someone in this building did. Why not Tad?" Estebe rubbed the top of his head.

Angie felt the challenge in Estebe's words. So instead of responding, she glanced around the room. "We don't just pick the easiest target. We need to know who was in on this."

"Sorry, that was an overreaction. Which was still better than what I wanted to say." He stood from the bench and stretched. "I'm tired. Words seem to be coming out of my mouth on their own terms. And I hate charlatans."

"Gift horses and all," Matt provided.

"Exactly." Estebe slapped Matt on the back. "Thanks buddy."

Angie wasn't sure where this conversation had gone off the rails, but it was obvious that everyone was tired and needed some sleep. She glanced around. The guards still weren't back. "Let's go find Bridget, and then we're going to the closest cells and getting a few hours of sleep. One of us will stay awake just in case."

"We could switch off every hour." Matt added. He yawned, rubbing his eyes.

"I'll take the first watch." Ian nodded to the bank of cells near the back of the room. "I'll wait for our hosts to come back. You all go get some sleep. Who wants second shift?"

Felicia raised her hand. "I'm good with cat naps."

"Let's do two on guard. I'll sit up with Ian first. Then Ian will go to bed and I'll stay up with Felicia. Then I'll go to bed and Felicia can sit with the next person." Angie suggested. "That way it's less likely that our guard will fall asleep too."

"Hey, I might resemble that remark." Ian smiled at her. "But it's a good call. I'm drained and this way, I have someone to talk to."

"Then put me on the third shift," Nancy said. "With having two jobs that will be just about the time I'm used to getting up anyway."

"That would bring us up to the unlock time. Then we just have to stop for coffee and get home so we can open on time tomorrow." Estebe looked at his watch. "Or technically, today."

"See you all in the morning," Ian called as he refilled his coffee cup. He held up an empty cup, "Want some?"

"Yes, please." Angie met him at the coffee pot.

They took the coffee and followed the group to the bank of cells. There was a table close and Ian sat with his back to the cells, watching the front.

Angie pointed to the cell block. "Should we walk through before they go to sleep to make sure no one's there?"

"Estebe was going to do that before he laid down."

Angie eyed him suspiciously. "And how do you know that?"

"We talked with sign language when I was pouring coffee. He's not a stupid man. He worries about you guys." Ian sipped his coffee. "And before you ask, there isn't an exit to the back. I went through this set of cells earlier trying to find the bathroom. It's on the other side. This blocks up to a brick wall."

"I can't believe we're worried about getting killed in our sleep. This was supposed to be a fun, teambuilding activity. Maybe I should schedule all the others. We could go to the zoo. That would be safe, right?"

"Until a lion escapes and we're stuck hiding in the monkey house." He shook his head. "Face it Angie, wherever you go, trouble shows up. I think you have a natural attraction for problems."

"This is really not my fault." Angie saw the grin on Ian's face. "Okay, so you're teasing me."

"And you didn't catch on for a while. You are tired." Ian glanced around the common room. At the other end of the room, the two couples were sitting up against a wall, with either one or both of the pair sleeping. Tamera had her head on the table, snoring. Tad was pacing the room. And Thaddeus was still playing cards. "I think our hosts found beds and are asleep by now."

"You don't think the guards killed Pat, do you?"

Ian glanced over at the others one more time. "Either one of them did, or it's someone over there. Would a killer be asleep right now? Or would he be filled with adrenaline and not able to sleep?"

"He'd have to be pretty cold blooded to sleep." She watched Tad. "He's wound a little tightly for someone his age."

"Unless you add in the time he spent in lock up. He's probably thinking he's the most likely candidate for suspect of the year." Ian rolled his shoulders. "When I was running with Danny, everyone thought I was doing the same bad things he was. And I like it that way. It gave me street cred, but I was a dumb kid. Tad *knows* what it's like to go to prison. I don't think he's very keen on going back."

"You empathize with him." Angie watched Ian's face. The room was gloomy but she could see him clear enough.

"I do. I could have been Danny or Tad if my mom hadn't stepped in. She saved me from a bad turn in life by just taking me out of town that weekend." He nodded to Tad. "You never know what could have happened if someone had interceded in his life. Like a favorite uncle."

"Sometimes people won't let you help." Angie didn't mean to be critical of Ian's choices, but she'd tried to save others before. It never worked out.

"You're right. I believe all we can do is try." He smiled at her. "Of course, I am the Sunday school teacher. I'm required to say this kind of stuff."

"Whatever." Angie put her elbows on the table and leaned forward. Dom looked up at her and barked. "Uh oh, we need to find the courtyard. Dom's needing a break."

"I don't want you to go alone." Ian glanced over at the cells. "Anyone still awake in there?"

Marty popped his head up and moved toward the entrance. "I can't sleep. I've been trying but my head keeps running through the people we met and any reasons they might have wanted to kill Pat. How can I help?"

"Go with Angie to find the courtyard. Dom needs a walk." Ian handed Matt one of the flashlights that were on the table.

They walked toward the hallway that led even farther into the prison. Angie shivered and Matt shined the light on her. "You okay?"

"I'm fine, it's just a little weird, that's all." She rubbed the top of Dom's back. More for her own comfort than the dog's. "Thanks for coming with me."

"I like working for you. I need to keep you around. Estebe and Felicia together would be brutal." He pointed toward a door with a sign that read *Exercise Yard*. "I think we found our exit."

"Just make sure there's a rock or something in the doorway. I would hate to get locked outside for the rest of the night." Angie and Dom moved through the doorway. The night was cool, but not cold. And the walls were high enough that all Angie could see were the stars above them. "This is amazing."

"Yeah. I know we're close to town but you'd think we were out in the boonies here." He shoved a rock in the door. He kicked a coffee can and sand flew out of it. "Looks like people take smoke breaks out here."

"What do you think of Glen, Marty, and Bridget?" Angie let Dom loose on his leash to find the perfect spot. She was glad when he decided it was just time to water the lawn. She didn't want to have to pull out her pooper scooper bags, carry his refuse back inside and dump it in the toilet. Sometimes being a responsible pet owner wasn't a fun job.

"I'm worried about them. Yeah, they are probably just sleeping on couches in the break room, but what if they aren't? I hate to think that the killer got them too." He glanced toward the door. "I messed up by booking this thing. Next time, it's a trip to POJO's Fun Palace where the hardest thing is laser tag."

"Matt, this is not on you. You couldn't predict a murder. And unless you killed the guy, you're not responsible for his death." Dom sat at her feet, watching her. "I need to get him some water anyway. Let's go visit the break room."

"Sounds like a plan." He held open the door and they went from the gentle star light into pitch black. Matt flipped on the flashlight. "I can't believe how dark it is in here."

"We got used to it." Angie tried to stay in the middle of the walkway, not that she was afraid of random hands and arms reaching out and grabbing her from the dark shadows. At least, not very afraid. They paused at the table where Ian sat.

"Everything okay?" Ian greeted Dom as he talked, rubbing the big dog's ears.

"Sure. We need to get the big guy some water so he can go out again." Angie grabbed a plastic bowl from the middle of the table. It held candy, but was almost empty now. "We'll be right back."

She didn't mention that they were looking for the three missing hosts as well, but she didn't think Ian would be fooled. He could read her like a book sometimes. They wandered through the empty display rooms until they reached the one that had posters of all the famous inmates.

"This is totally creepy in the dark. It's like they're all looking at you." Matt shined the light on all of the posters.

"Then stop with the light stuff. Shine it on this wall. I thought I saw a door here earlier."

Sure enough, there was a door marked *Staff Only*. Angie opened the door and they went inside. There were tables, couches, vending machines, and a fridge, but no people. It was completely empty.

"Okay, so where are they?" Matt rechecked the room, shining the light in all the corners.

Angie moved to the sink to fill Dom's bowl. She sat it on the floor and looked around while he slurped it up. "I don't know."

A banging from the right side of the room made her jump. "Matt, shine your light over there."

When he did, they saw a new door. Matt whistled and said, "It appears the banging is coming from there."

Angie glanced around the room and picked up an empty vase. She moved around Dom who was still drinking and toward the door. "Okay, you open the door and I'll hit them with the vase."

Matt nodded and they moved slowly toward the door. When they got there, they realized the outside had a latch on it. He pulled the latch slowly aside and pulled open the door.

Three people fell out of the small closet. Glen was the first to stand up. When he saw Angie's upstretched hands holding the vase, he gently took it away from her. "Thank god you came looking for us. We've been locked in that closet for hours."

"Don't exaggerate, Glen." Bridget looked at her watch. "Okay, maybe it was a couple of hours. It felt like eternity. What's been going on?"

Matt shrugged. "Not much. We've got a group sleeping. And the others are sitting and waiting. No new murders."

Dom barked his opinion.

Marty dusted his pants off as he stood up. Then he went to the fridge and opened the door. "I'm dying of thirst."

"Hand me a cola." Bridget said as she sat down at the table. "All of my muscles hurt from being shoved in there."

"Who locked you up?"

The three of them looked at each other. Bridget finally answered the question. "You're not going to believe this but he wore an executioner's hood. It has to be the one in the display room for the gallows."

"But you knew it was a he?" Angie pressed. Maybe there were clues that would limit the number of suspects.

"Yeah. Well, I guess I thought it was a man. He held a knife and motioned us into the closet. Then I heard him rummaging around the room." Bridget looked up and smiled at Marty. Marty sat cold drinks in front of her and Glen, who joined them at the table.

"This is supposed to be an acting job. You tell the stories, give the tour, then watch until people leave in the morning. No one said I was going to be locked up in a broom closet." Glen opened his soda with a crack. "I'm beginning to think I need to look for another job."

"Don't jump too soon. This job is fine. Well, as long as no one gets killed. And besides, we don't know that Pat's death had anything to do with the prison. Maybe one of those people out there had it in for him. The guy could be a real butt." Bridget put a hand on Glen's and Angie saw a look pass between the two.

"Well, I'm glad we found you. We were beginning to worry." Angie nodded to the door. "We're going back to the great room. What about you guys? Are you staying in here?"

"Why, so we can get locked up again? I think not." Marty grabbed a soda out of the fridge and nodded to the door. "Come on lovebirds, let's go join the group."

Angie smiled as she walked back out to the common room. She'd been right about Glen and Bridget. They were involved. There were many connections within the group. Glen and Bridget, Marty and Pat's ex-wife, Marty and Pat. Was it that simple? Had Marty killed Pat in a fit of rage? She shook her head, ending the mental gymnastics. Marty just didn't fit the killer mold. At least in her mind. This would be one investigation she'd love turning over to the police just as soon the doors opened later that morning.

The guards/hosts were met by a round of welcomes and where have you beens. Angie and Dom moved over to the table where Ian sat watching them.

"So you found the missing few." He nodded to the guards who were now talking to an agitated Tad. "That guy is going to give himself a heart attack if he's not careful."

"Once we're out of here, it's not our problem." She sat next to Ian. Dom inched under the table and laid down with his head on her foot. "Anything interesting happen here while I was gone?"

"Not a thing. Except Estebe snores like he's cutting logs back there."

Angie glanced back at the cells, grimacing. "He gets up super early and goes to work out at one of those 24/7 gyms. Then he does his real estate investing stuff. Then he comes to work. And, I hear he spends a few hours a week volunteering with the Basque Community Center Men's group. The guy is always moving."

"He makes me look like a slacker." Ian grinned. "No wonder I like the guy. We're poster children for Over Achievers Anonymous."

"You balance me out nicely." Angie rubbed his arm and laid her head on his shoulder.

Ian chuckled. "You? You're the president. You've had not one but two successful restaurants straight out of college. You don't do that if you're a slacker, and you are no slacker."

She thought about her old boyfriend and former partner in el Pescado, her first restaurant. He'd been a slacker, but he'd picked two over achievers for partners. And he walked away with a large profit from that first venture for very little work.

Angie and Ian played cards for the rest of the time. Finally, he glanced at his watch. "Sorry to leave you, but I've got to get some z's. Do you want me to wake up Felicia?"

"Let her sleep for fifteen more minutes." Angie glanced at her watch. "I can handle a few minutes alone. I promise I'll wake her up right at the hour."

"You better." He kissed the top of her head. "See you later today."

Angie focused on the game of Solitaire she spread out before her. But then she heard a noise. Thinking it was Felicia, she didn't look up. She pulled her sweater close as the air seemed chilly. "I was going to wake you in five minutes. How'd you sleep?"

When Felicia didn't answer, Angie looked up and saw Nancy staring at her. "Go back to bed. You have another hour to sleep."

"I didn't mean for this to happen. The one that acted is not acting in my name." Nancy said.

Frowning, Angie looked up from her cards. Nancy looked pale under the low light. "What are you talking about? You feeling okay?"

"The first murder was my fault. I was angry. He got me pregnant then promised I'd be able to keep the baby. You heard the story." Nancy laughed, but there was no humor in the laugh. "Then when she was gone, I broke. My heart broke. You have to believe me. I didn't want this. This is an abomination."

A chill ran down Angie's spine. "Wait, you're not Nancy, are you? Lyda? Is that you?"

"You are wise beyond your years. I watch. I see." Nancy reached down to Dom who was watching her from under the table. "You are kind to animals and feed others. You have to step in and stop him. I'm afraid if he gets away with this, the madness will keep him killing."

Angie glanced down at Dom. He was not growling at the "not Nancy" person, but he wasn't wagging his tail in welcome either. He seemed as confused as she felt. "Okay. So you killed the original guard way back when. Why did someone kill Pat? Was it because of the first murder?"

Not Nancy shook her head slowly. "No. This was just blood lust. You must stop him. Stop him. Stop him. Stop him."

Chapter 7

With each sentence, Nancy's voice got louder and louder. "Stop him."

Finally, Tad yelled from the other side of the room. "Shut up. It's bad enough we're stuck in here without someone yelling about some dog."

Apparently, Tad misinterpreted Lyda's intended target for the words, but his voice silenced her. When Angie looked up, Nancy was standing in front of her, looking dazed and tired.

"Is it time for me to watch now? I feel like I just barely laid down." She glanced around the room, confusion on her face.

"Go back to bed. You're about an hour early." Angie put a hand on Nancy's back and led her back to her bunk. Then she woke up Felicia.

When she joined Felicia at the table, Angie told her about what happened with Nancy.

"And you're sure she wasn't just messing with you, right?" Felicia sipped the fresh coffee she'd just poured into a Styrofoam cup. "They really need better coffee. Maybe I'll send them a bag of ours once we get out of here."

"Seriously? A ghost possesses one of our friends to talk to me about a murder, and all you can think about is coffee?" Angie leaned back and watched Felicia. "What exactly would excite you? A nuclear bomb blast?"

"Give me a break. It's early. I tend to sleep in, especially since I'm so wound up when we finish service it's hard for me to relax right away." She sipped her coffee. "I don't think she gave you any information that we didn't have already."

"She said he thought he was working for her. Why would anyone try to defend the honor of a long dead woman?"

They sat quietly for a while. Finally, Felicia spoke. "You wouldn't. Unless you were freaking crazy. Or..."

Angie nodded, following Felicia's trail. "Or you were related to her. Hatfield's and McCoy's type of feud. She said the baby was a girl. And we know the baby was taken away from her just after birth. Would that baby still be alive?"

"Possibly. According to the poster, Lyda was released in 1941. Depending on when this happened, the baby might be in her early eighties?"

Angie pursed her lips together, thinking. "Well we don't have any eighty-year-olds on the tour, so a kid would be in their what? Sixties?"

"And that we *do* have on the tour. Thaddeus. He's got to be in his sixties or older."

They looked over at the old man who was still playing with the cards, ignoring everything around him. Felicia shook her head. "I don't know. He doesn't look strong enough to stick someone with a knife."

"Go down a generation. Maybe Tad is doing his uncle a favor by defending great grandma's honor?" Angie watched the still pacing Tad cross the room.

"Doesn't quite fit somehow. Tamera's still asleep. She'd have to be awfully cold to sleep like that next to the dead body." Felicia yawned. "Well, the good thing is that the police will be here soon and take all this wondering off our plate. Unless you plan on having the case solved before they even get into the building."

"Would be nice, but I don't have a clue who killed Pat. And if we count Lyda as a credible source, she said he. Not she." Angie rubbed her eyes. "I wish I had my laptop. I could look up all the players and see if something just felt off."

"Investigations via Google, I like it. Although we're kind of stuck with the old-fashioned method here. Maybe that's why Lyda's ghost came to visit. She knew we were in the dark, so to speak." Felicia grinned. "We're going to have to call you the ghost whisperer."

"Please don't. That was spooky. You didn't see the change on Nancy's face." Angie shivered at the memory. She was quiet for a minute. "Okay, so who are our main suspects? Thaddeus, Tad, and Marty?"

"I'm not certain Glen's off the list." Felicia added. "The other two guys, Nick and Jamie, have been with their new wives this entire time. Sara's trying to get Nick to give up the ghost hunting life, and Liz, she's as deep into it as Jamie. I think all of them are off the list."

"Marriage is hard enough without going it trying to change someone to who you want them to be. What chance do you think they have?"

"It depends on how much he loves her." Glen sat down at the table with them. "Sorry, you two are the only ones awake and talking. Both Marty and Bridget finally went down a few minutes ago."

Felicia and Angie exchanged glances. "No problem. We find talking helps pass the time. You spent time with the newlyweds, what do you think?"

"I agree. Nick and Sara won't make it. But the other two just might. You have to have something in common. That's why Pat and Rachel blew up. He liked spending his time at the bar when he was off. Rachel wanted a little house and picket fence. Marty gave her that even though they are still just dating." Glen rolled his shoulders. "The tour nights are long. I've had a lot of time to talk with both of them."

"Would Marty have killed Pat?" Angie decided to keep the guy talking.

"You're kidding, right? Marty doesn't have a mean bone in his body. Sure, he'd defend himself, but Pat wouldn't have charged him. He would have gone and messed with Rachel's head if he'd really wanted her back. It was all just posturing for him. He didn't want her but he wasn't sure he wanted her to be happy with another guy."

"You seem to know a lot about all the players here."

He grinned as he finished his coffee. "I'm finishing up my degree in psychology. I'm a people watcher. I'm writing a book on how weird we all are and ways to manage each type. You two are problem solvers. You protect your group by getting everyone together and in a safe place, then you stand watch. I would have thought your men would be the ones out here but no, they are both asleep. You have no skin in the game here, yet you are trying to figure out the killer."

"We do have skin in the game, as you say," Angie knew he'd heard all of their conversation then, including the part where he'd been one of the suspects. "We're locked in here with a killer."

"True. But you didn't have to come looking for us when we were locked up. Which by the way, doesn't that take both me and Marty off the suspect list? We didn't lock ourselves up in a closet for hours." Glen stood and held up his cup. "Anyone want a refill?"

"I'm good." Felicia said as Angie shook her head.

When he was out of earshot, Angie leaned over. "He's right. Unless they have a partner, none of those three could have done it. We're down to Tad and Thaddeus. Unless he had a partner."

"You said that already." Felicia turned her head and watched Angie, who had her head turned toward the others in the room. "What are you looking for?"

Angie nodded toward Sara. "That. She's watching Glen and they just made eye contact. How tall do you think she is?"

"Almost five nine if I'm remembering right, why?"

"What if she's the partner that shoved Glen into the closet so he could have an alibi? Who talked to her?"

"Hope, why?" Felicia studied the girl who was now watching as Glen returned to the guard's table where the other two still were asleep.

"Because I wonder if she's a student at Boise State, and what her major is."

Chapter 8

Angie didn't go back to sleep. She stayed up with Felicia and they talked about everything and nothing as they kept their eyes on Glen and Sara. When Estebe woke, they filled him in on their suspicions. He glanced around the room. "I'm uncomfortable having our team sleeping when we know there is a murderer in the room. I know I suggested it in the first place, but maybe we should waken them and talk to Hope?"

Angie shook her head. "Right now, it's all speculation. I guess a crime scene tech might be able to prove that Glen's fingerprints were on the knife, or that Sara wore the executioner's hood, but right now, it's all suspicion."

"So what? We're just going to tell the cops our theory?" Felicia snorted. "I don't think they care about reasoning. Pat's dead and Marty is probably going to be charged with his murder."

"I think that's the plan all along. Sara needed a job that would be interesting for Nick in the area. He was talking about starting a traveling paranormal podcast with Jamie and Liz. If they had a spot here, he wouldn't pass up working at one of the most haunted sites in Boise. And she wouldn't have to leave the area." Angie paused, her eyes brightening. "We need to hold a séance."

"You have got to be kidding." Felicia touched Angie's forehead. "No fever so why are you talking crazy?"

"We need to get everyone together, then we can force Sara or Glen to confess." She tapped the table. "It's the only way. And if I bring in the info we got from our friendly ghost, it should throw them off guard. Especially if we focus on Nick being the killer."

Estebe nodded. "Then Sara will say something stupid to save him?"

"What? That plan worked on all the *Scooby Doo* mysteries." Angie grinned. "And if it doesn't, it passes the time and the cops will be here to take over. It's a win, win."

"Unless Glen gets worried and kills you." Felicia pointed out.

"If we're all together, he'd have to kill everyone. This keeps us all safe. We're each other's witnesses." Angie shrugged. "Anyone else have a better plan? If not, go wake the others, tell them what we've got going, and I'll get the rest of the cast in on the play. If anything, it won't be boring."

When Angie crossed the room, she started with Liz. Liz and Jamie believed in the supernatural so they would be the easiest to convince and might even have some experience running one. Angie hadn't guessed wrong.

"OMG. Why didn't I think of that? You are brilliant. We need to hurry because as soon as the sun rises, Lyda will be gone until next year. She probably knows who killed the guard too. Ghosts have more information than we do. They see everything." Liz shook her husband. "Go wake everyone. We'll set up on the long table in the middle of the room."

Angie let Liz take the lead. That way, she could watch how everyone reacted. As she'd suspected, Sara was hard to convince but Nick pulled her along. When Jamie got to the guards' station, he used their knowledge against them.

"We need you all to verify the facts. Sometimes people try to use these situations for their own gains. If one of us is a murderer, they could twist the history and pretend to have a message from the other side. You all know the history of at least this place. You can keep this honest." Jamie pleaded with them. "And it keeps us all busy until the doors open. It's kind of your job, man."

Angie saw the calculations running through Glen's head as he decided how to play this twist. She wondered what he'd call Jamie. A persuader?

Within twenty minutes, the stage was set. They were all gathered around the table. Liz opened the discussion with a call for them all to join hands and for the spirit world to open its doors. "If anyone has had a visitation this night from a spirit, please tell us the message you received."

"I got a message." Angie spoke calmly. "Lyda visited me through the body of my friend, Nancy."

"What are you talking about?" Nancy shook her head. "I don't remember this."

"You were probably in a dream trance." Liz quietly explained. "Let Angie tell us the message."

Angie could feel everyone's eyes on her. "Lyda said the murder was a mistake. That someone was acting in her memory and that he was wrong to try to enact revenge on an innocent man."

Marty snorted. "Well, we know this is bunk because Pat wasn't innocent. He was a mean jerk and used people."

"I don't think that was what she was talking about. She said she'd killed the prison guard in anger because her daughter had been taken from her. She said she was wrong to strike out but that whoever killed Pat was related to her and acting unwisely." Angie glanced at Thaddeus.

"How the hell did you figure that out?" He rubbed his face. "You're right and you're wrong. I am descended from Lyda. From that baby girl that was taken from her. But I didn't kill the guard. I was here to try to contact her. To see if those rumors about her haunting this place were true. To show her that we'd made a difference with our lives. Lives that she gave us."

"What are you talking about?" Tamera stared at her uncle. "This is why you wanted to come here? To talk to a dead person rather than bond with Tad and me?"

He shook his head with a slight eye roll. "You two are fine. Your space in the will is set. You won't be left penniless."

"It's not about the money." Tad shot back. "You're the closest thing I've had to a father since I was sixteen and you treat us like we're strangers. Why can't you just be a normal uncle and take us to dinner. Ask what's going on in our lives? Just give a shit."

"Tad," Tamera squeezed her brother's hand.

"No, he's right. I've been distant. At first, I thought you were okay. You didn't need me. Then I just lost track. I focused on my career and the money and not the people who matter. I'm sorry." Thaddeus took put his hand on the top of the siblings'.

"Touching family scene aside, which one of you two killed Pat?" Bridget brought the conversation back to the present. "The ghost said one of you did it for the wrong reasons."

"I didn't kill your friend. I was here for other reasons." Thaddeus glanced at his nephew. "And I believe Tad was here to please me."

"I didn't kill anyone. I might be a screw up, but I'm not an idiot." Tad broke the circle and wiped his eyes. "So find another patsy. I'm not being one this time."

"Return to the circle." Liz commanded. And to Angie's surprise, Tad followed suit.

Angie spoke up. "She didn't say a relative did this, she said someone did it in her name. Someone killed Pat because he was like the guard who fathered her child."

"I'm telling you all again, I didn't kill Pat." Marty sighed. "Did I hate the guy? Yes. Was he making Rachel's life hell because she was in love with me? Yes. Did I want him out of our lives? Hell, yes."

"There's one person who would benefit from this chaos. There's one person who needed Pat out of the way." Angie shook her head at Marty who started to speak. "It was you Sara. You killed Pat so Nick could take his job."

"That's stupid. Sara didn't even know I wanted to work here. Besides, we've got a gig in the works. The four of us are starting a ghost busting podcast. It's going to be awesome." Nick turned and looked at his new wife who was staring at Angie, her face pale. "Right, honey? Honey?"

"Stop talking about that dumb podcast. It's not going to make a dime. How do you plan on us making rent or even putting gas in that dumpy van of yours? And you're running our credit cards up with your stupid toys." The words fell out of Sara's mouth before she realized what she was saying.

"You killed someone?" Nick stared at her.

"No. I didn't. Honey, look, I just want us to be okay. I want you to think about us, not this stupid podcast." She looked pleadingly at her new husband. Then she looked at the table. "I didn't kill Pat."

"But someone did, and you helped him." Angie repeated. "Do you want to tell us why you locked the guards in the closet?"

She stared at Angie. "How did you know that was me?"

"You stupid cow." Glen yelled at her. "They were guessing and now you've just gone and ruined my alibi. I should have known you weren't up to this. You're a B student at most."

"Hey, I'm Dean's List, just like you." Sara shot back. "I wrote most of your damn book."

"And now you've ruined the whole thing." Glen stood up and pulled a gun out of the back of his pants. "I guess it's going to have to be a Halloween massacre story. Thank God I wrestled the gun away from him before crazy Tad took us all out. Thanks for the poor little rich boy story. That will help with the motivation."

"I don't think so." A man spoke behind where Glen stood. "Lower your weapon or you will be the first down."

Angie looked up into the face of Sheriff Allen Brown, Ian's uncle. He and several other law enforcement officers stood with guns drawn all focused on Glen's back.

"How did he know?" She whispered to Ian.

"Beats me, but I'm glad he's here."

Chapter 9

Angie and the crew gathered around the table where they'd eaten dinner. It seemed so long ago. She sank into a bench to watch as the police first brought out Glen and Sara to patrol cars, then Pat's body to the coroner's wagon. A small woman pulled up in a Mini Cooper and ran towards Marty. She didn't even glance at the cart while it wheeled her ex-husband to the wagon. Angie watched as Rachel threw her arms around the clearly tired Marty. "True love always wins."

Ian followed her gaze and smiled. Then he stepped forward to talk to his uncle. "Are we free to go? Or do we need to hang around longer?"

Allen Brown took out a handkerchief and mopped at his face. "You can go. We know where to find you in case there are more questions. Miss Turner, I can't believe you got yourself into another situation here. Didn't we just talk about this?"

"Don't look at me. I didn't schedule this outing, Matt did." She rubbed her face. She needed sleep before service tonight. "Hey, how did you know we were in trouble? The doors were supposed to open at six, which was only fifteen minutes ago."

"Oh, yeah, I forgot to tell you. Your goat got out of her pen."

Angie's heart missed a beat. Visions of the trucks that sped down the road in front of her house filled her head. "Precious? Tell me she's okay."

"She's fine. Erica called me to tell you that she took her over to the goat farm since she didn't know how to fix your fence. She's heading out of town to visit with her parents, so she wanted to make sure someone knew where Precious was. I tried to call the emergency line so I could get a message to you, but it was off line. That phone is always supposed to be open. So the security company checked an open feed to the common room, and that female guard kept staring at the camera and mouthing SOS. When Glen would walk by, she'd pretend to be sleeping. So we had a pretty good understanding of what was going on about an hour ago. We just had to get people here. Once Glen started talking mass killing, we knew we were out of time."

"Precious saved us?" Angie started giggling.

Allen exchanged looks with Ian. "I said all of that and all she heard was her goat saved you?"

"She's had a long night." He slapped Allen on the back. "We're taking off. I've got to get her home so she can get some sleep, or no one's eating at the County Seat tonight. Besides, it sounds like I have a fence to mend."

They said their goodbyes but as they were leaving the area, a school bus stopped at the gate to the penitentiary. The teacher was trying to figure out who to talk to with the police and ambulances blocking the way.

"I think their Halloween party just got cancelled." Ian looked up at the kids hanging out of the windows, staring at the building.

"I bet a lot of people died in there," one little boy said to his friend.

The other one pointed to the door, "Look, there's a real live prisoner standing at the doorway. Maybe she escaped."

Angie turned to see a woman dressed in a 1940's traveling suit. She held a suitcase. She smiled at Angie and nodded her head. Then she looked up and disappeared.

"Wicked cool. Did you see that? She was a ghost. And not one of those stupid sheet covered people. I bet she's a hologram. Do you think she'll run on a loop?"

Angie knew that what she'd seen hadn't been a special effect. Lyda had left the building. And it was about time. Angie stood there a minute longer, watching the place where Lyda had been standing.

"Angie, do you need me to go get the car? You can sit on that bench and I'll be right back." Ian took her arm.

"I'm fine. I was just looking at something." Angie fell into step with Ian. It was time to get back to the real world. A world where long dead people didn't use her staff members as their personal Western Union. "Time to start thinking about what we're cooking tonight. If you want to come by, I'll buy your dinner."

"Sounds amazing."

They walked hand in hand down the short hill to the parking lot. Then she got into Ian's car and leaned her head against the window. She closed her eyes and stopped thinking of Lyda altogether.

Dear Readers,

Muffins are the first thing I learned to bake in Mrs. Higgin's Freshman Home Ec class. I think I still have the apron I made in that class, sharing fabric with my best friend and her sister. High school is where I became aware of the possibilities of being an adult. Having my own place, making my own meals. It all seemed so magical then. I dreamt of being a fashion buyer in New York City (I would have never loved the heels), or a suited lawyer fighting for the rights of others, or a mom with twelve kids making muffins and serving on the PTA.

Instead, I had one kid, one career in social service, now one in the private sector, and finally, the dream job I never thought I could have – author. Follow your dreams because you can't change the past, but you can always start over and change the future.

Much love,
Lynn

Special Chocolate Chip Muffins

Pre-heat oven to 400 degrees. Grease 12 muffin tins (or use spray oil). Mix into a large bowl

2 cups all-purpose flour
1⁄3 cup light-brown sugar, packed
1⁄3 cup sugar
2 teaspoons baking powder
1⁄2 teaspoon salt

In a separate bowl, mix

2⁄3 cup milk
1⁄2 cup butter, melted and cooled
2 eggs, lightly beaten
1 teaspoon vanilla

Make a well in the middle of the dry ingredients and pour in the wet ingredients. Mix together, but don't over mix. (Rookie mistake I've made too many times.)

Add to the mix

1 (11 1/2 ounce) package semi-sweet chocolate chips
1⁄2 cup walnuts, chopped
1/2 cup dried cranberries

Pour into muffin tins and bake for 15-20 minutes. Let cool.

Love the Farm-to-Fork Mysteries?

Don't miss the rest of the series

WHO MOVED MY GOAT CHEESE?

ONE POTATO, TWO POTATO, DEAD

KILLER GREEN TOMATOES

DEEP FRIED REVENGE

And novella

HAVE A DEADLY NEW YEAR

Available now

And be sure to read these mystery series by Lynn Cahoon

The Cat Latimer Mysteries

The Tourist Trap Mysteries

And coming soon

The Kitchen Witch Mysteries!

Printed in the United States
by Baker & Taylor Publisher Services